First Summer

First Summer

Ekin Oklap

Summit
Books

London · New York · Amsterdam/Antwerp · Sydney/Melbourne · Toronto · New Delhi

Summit
Books

First published in Great Britain by Summit Books,
an imprint of Simon & Schuster UK Ltd, 2026

First published in the United States by Summit Books,
an imprint of Simon & Schuster LLC, 2026

1 3 5 7 9 10 8 6 4 2

Simon & Schuster UK Ltd, 1st Floor, 222 Gray's Inn Road
London WC1X 8HB

Simon & Schuster Australia, Sydney
Simon & Schuster India, New Delhi

www.simonandschuster.co.uk
www.simonandschuster.com.au
www.simonandschuster.co.in

The authorised representative in the EEA is Simon & Schuster Netherlands BV,
Herculesplein 96, 3584 AA Utrecht, Netherlands. info@simonandschuster.nl

A CIP catalogue record for this book is available from the British Library

Hardback ISBN: 978-1-3985-5158-9
Trade Paperback ISBN: 978-1-3985-5159-6
eBook ISBN: 978-1-3985-5160-2
Audio ISBN: 978-1-3985-5161-9

Typeset by Palimpsest Book Production Ltd, Falkirk, Stirlingshire
Printed and Bound in the UK using 100% Renewable Electricity at CPI Group (UK) Ltd

FSC
www.fsc.org
MIX
Paper | Supporting
responsible forestry
FSC® C013604

First Summer

1

It was so hot that summer that they kept talking about it on the news. During the day, the air was so thick with moisture that it was hard to breathe sometimes, and at night the bedsheets stuck to your skin like shrouds and made you dream strange dreams. People tried to carry on as normal, and for the most part, they managed; but as they went about their business and ran their daily errands, you could tell from the looks on their faces that they all thought this was no way to live, and that they would much rather hibernate their way through the worst of it.

In that summer of wet hot days and restless nights, a girl I had never seen before moved into the brown house at the end of the road. She arrived one day, seemingly out of nowhere, in the back of a blue car that moved slowly up the road as if the driver were unsure where to stop. When it finally reached the brown house, the car nearly drove straight past it, braking abruptly only when Old Mrs Dickie – who must have been watching from behind the curtains – flung the front door open and waved. The girl and the driver got out and started unloading her things. Old Mrs Dickie went back into the house, then re-emerged to hand something to the driver. I saw him nod at her and carry the girl's luggage – two mismatched suitcases and a small red holdall – into the house while Old Mrs Dickie held the door open and the girl waited outside, her backpack against her chest.

After the driver was gone, Old Mrs Dickie and the girl stood staring at each other for a moment. Then Old Mrs Dickie smiled. The girl smiled back, though because of the distance, I couldn't really tell whether she meant it. Then she did something strange: she held out her hand to Old Mrs Dickie, who shook it. The strangeness was not so much in the handshake itself, but in the fact that it was the girl who'd initiated it.

Old Mrs Dickie ushered her inside and closed the door behind them both. I watched it all from my spot out on our porch, feeling as if I had melted into the rocking chair, and trying to trick my mind into believing in a breeze that wasn't there. I had already spent many summer hours in that chair; I was often alone, and there wasn't much else to do. But there I could read undisturbed, and drink lemonade, and chew on ice cubes. It made me feel like there was nothing more I needed.

I sat cratered in the rocking chair for another hour, but the girl did not come back out, and eventually, my mother called me in for dinner. I must have been asleep when she got back, because I hadn't seen her come home. Even at that hour it was still so hot that I could barely eat, though I knew I should since my mother had taken the trouble to cook. As always, she seemed preoccupied with something other than me. I told myself, if she looks up from her plate or away from the old TV in our kitchen, if she asks me a question, any question, then I will eat everything she's put on my plate. I counted ten minutes exactly – I could tell from the clock next to the fridge – but she said nothing. I thought that maybe she hated me, so I finished my food anyway, because I wanted her to know how wrong she was.

2

Joe came by on his new bicycle the next day. He was my only friend in the neighbourhood, though it hadn't always been that way; he had once been one of a small group of boys I used to see nearly every day when I was much younger and school was out for summer. We would ride around on our bikes and spend afternoons at the public swimming pool, where we would soak for hours in the lukewarm water. I had almost nothing in common with these boys except for the time we shared, and sometimes they said things and made jokes that made me think they must also be spending time together without me, time in which they had more fun because I wasn't there. I didn't know this for sure, but I believed my suspicions to be reasonable, and in any case even the thought of it was bad enough. So I tried very hard to make them like me, and it seemed to work most of the time. Until one summer one of the managers at the pool called my mother to tell her that someone had complained about my swimming without a top on, like a boy. They had turned a blind eye so far, they said, because it hadn't really mattered when we were all still kids, but perhaps it was no longer appropriate now that we were getting older, so would she mind making sure I wore a proper bathing suit in the future?

I was watching from the kitchen table when my mother took this call. I did not know then who was calling and what about, but she was so embarrassed that I could tell it must be something bad. After she hung up, she looked at me for several seconds, then left without another word and came back forty-five minutes later with a one-piece bathing suit she told me I needed to start wearing if I wanted to keep going to the public pool; I was too old now to still be running around half-naked. The swimsuit was purple with a pink hem, and it fitted me perfectly. I liked it; I liked the way I looked in it, and I was pleased to have something new to show off to the boys. The next day, when they didn't cycle past my house as they usually did, I went to the pool by myself. When I got there, I could tell they had already been swimming without me all morning. I went over to their end of the pool but they barely acknowledged my arrival, except for Joe, who had always been the nicest to me. He told me he liked my new bathing suit. I left half an hour later, feeling mortified. They must have known about the complaint. There was no other explanation for why they seemed unable to look at me all of a sudden. It was as if my mother's embarrassment had been too great for her body alone to contain; some of it had spilled over and into me, and from there spread to the boys. Perhaps if I had pushed through the embarrassment, if I had kept following them around until they had no choice but to look at me again, things would have gone back to normal. But I didn't. I never went back to the pool, and quickly outgrew the purple bathing suit.

But all that had happened a long time ago. I was sixteen now, and Joe, who was a few months younger than me, was the only one I still spoke to. We met up occasionally and wandered around town, eating ice cream and making uncharitable comments about the people we passed. Here he came now, cycling very fast; I watched him round the corner with his head bowed low over the handlebar until he came to a dramatic stop in front of the rocking chair. I put my book down.

'Did you hear there's a new girl who's moved into Old Mrs Dickie's house?' he said, shielding his eyes from the sun.

I nodded.

'Her name is Clara,' he said. 'She's sixteen.'

'How do you know? Have you spoken to her?'

He was balancing on his bike now, standing on the pedals, twisting the front wheel this way and that.

'Mum told me. She ran into Old Mrs Dickie yesterday. She said her granddaughter was coming to stay with her for a while because her parents are away on a business trip.'

He finally lost his balance and had to put his feet back down. He looked up at me, squinting.

'You need a hat,' I told him.

'Mum thinks the story about the business trip isn't true,' he continued. 'She says she heard from her friend who plays rummy with Old Mrs Dickie that there's more to it, but they're not sure what.'

'Maybe her parents got divorced and couldn't decide what to do with her.'

Joe lowered his eyes for a moment, then looked up again.

'Mum says we should go and introduce ourselves, since she's our age. Shall we go this afternoon?'

'You mean when you're back from seeing your

friends?' I replied, picking at a thread that had come loose from the hem of my T-shirt.

Joe didn't say anything and looked at the ground again. He was frowning now. I felt bad for making him feel bad, and stupid for still caring about something that had happened when we were children.

'Your mum just wants us to make friends with her so we can find out all the gossip,' I said, rolling my eyes at him. He laughed, looking relieved, then said goodbye and cycled away.

I fell asleep in the rocking chair and dreamed that I was playing tennis with the new girl. I couldn't see her face properly because the sun was in my eyes, but I knew it was her. She was wearing green shorts with white pockets, and white canvas shoes. I looked down at my own shoes, which were also made of white canvas. In the dream, I knew this to be significant. She seemed very serious, and every time I tried to ask her a question, she just smiled and shrugged, as if she couldn't hear me. Then the dream turned into something else; I can't remember what.

3

JOE DIDN'T come back that day, but he returned the next morning. I grabbed my bike and we cycled slowly towards Old Mrs Dickie's house. Among the neighbourhood kids, Old Mrs Dickie had a reputation for strangeness, though it is difficult now, as it was then, to identify what it was exactly that we felt was so odd about her. She was not outwardly unfriendly; she did not shout at children and teenagers for no discernible reason, nor did she seem to resent our existence. Even now that we were older, she still looked unspeakably ancient to us: yet unlike every other elderly person we knew, she seemed to need no help at all. She did her own shopping, mowed her own lawn, collected her own prescriptions, and that – accustomed as we were to old people depending to varying degrees on the help of others – seemed to suggest that something about her was not quite normal. The adults didn't notice, of course, and in retrospect she can't have been as old as we thought she was, for she had lived there longer than any of us had been alive, and looked almost exactly the same as when we were toddlers. Still, it wasn't without some trepidation that we approached her house that day, leaning our bikes against the wall before knocking softly on the door. She opened it almost immediately and was perfectly kind to us, betraying only the briefest hint of surprise at the explanation we offered for our visit. She led us into the living room and told us to wait while she went and fetched Clara.

We had never been inside Old Mrs Dickie's house, yet somehow it seemed familiar: the pattern on the wall-paper was slightly faded, the coffee table was scuffed in all the expected places and one end of the couch sunk lower than the other, revealing exactly where Old Mrs Dickie liked to sit when she watched TV. Then Clara walked into the room, and suddenly everything looked different, as if she had wandered in from another world and in doing so had brought a little of that world with her. It was like seeing a fox crossing the street in broad daylight. She looked exactly like a girl our age was supposed to look – a little taller, perhaps, but otherwise just like the rest of us, with spots on her chin and colourful, slightly ill-fitting clothes. No doubt there was the novelty of a stranger appearing in our midst, but I think there was also something about her in particular – how she was a little out of breath as she walked in, as if she had sprinted back inside, unable to contain her curiosity; the dark smudge on her forehead, which I assumed was dirt from the garden; the lopsided daisy chain in her hair.

'Hi,' she said with a small smile. I thought she looked sad, but perhaps she was just shy. 'I'm Clara. It's so nice of you to come by. I don't know anyone here.'

We introduced ourselves, and as she sat in the chair across from us, her legs crossed at the ankles, we started telling her about the neighbourhood. Joe told her about our local landmarks: the public pool, the ice-cream van that never left its spot; I told her to avoid the strange man who lived in the house next to the cemetery and was rumoured to carry his cat's ashes in his pocket wherever he went, even to the supermarket. She smiled again and told us they had a strange man too in their neighbourhood back home, who called himself a mage and was said to run seances on the first Tuesday of every month. He wore a cape every time he went out to walk his dog. Joe told her about his dog, Sheba, whose age remained mysterious, and whose particular mix of breeds no one had ever been able to determine. Of course Clara could come over and meet her; Sheba loved new people. But what about Old Mrs Dickie: was it true that she ate three raw eggs every day, and that she'd been a champion tennis player in high school? It took Clara a moment to figure out who we were talking about, and then she burst out laughing. How funny that people here should call her grandma that. Dickie had been her granddad's nickname; it must have stuck to Grandma after Granddad died, but nobody in the family called her that. Clara wasn't sure about the eggs, but it was true about the tennis. Grandma no longer played, of course, but she might still have her old rackets somewhere in the house. Maybe we could borrow them some time; Grandma wouldn't mind. We didn't even attempt to conceal our excitement at this suggestion. Our practical experience of tennis was non-existent, but we'd seen people play in tournaments on TV and in the boring black-and-white movies our parents sometimes liked to watch. How hard could it be to replicate what we had observed?

A clock chimed faintly in the hallway; Joe checked the time on his new watch, which he liked to look at every chance he got, and announced that he should probably go. He and his little sister had promised to help their mother with lunch; they were expecting their aunt and her two young children – Joe's cousins – at noon. Suddenly Clara seemed sad again, her eyes shifting to her lap, her lips weighing down the corners of her mouth. 'I can stay,' I said without thinking. Clara turned to look at me and smiled, and it was so bright that it prickled my skin, like when you sit in a car that's been out in the sun for too long. Clara saw Joe out, and when she came back into the living room she took his spot at the sunken end of the sofa and started talking.

*

I learned many things about Clara that first day at Old Mrs Dickie's house. She had a long laugh, paired with an upward tilt of the eyebrows which made her look as if what she had just heard was the funniest and the most surprising thing anyone had ever said to her. She laughed often and easily, made you feel you were the cleverest, wittiest person she had ever met, and there was nothing else she'd rather be doing than talking to you.

I also learned that Clara was lonely. She never used that word, but every now and then she would say something that I would recognize so completely as a mirror of my own experience that it seemed almost unbelievable. When she told me that she didn't really understand her classmates, I knew what she actually meant: that she didn't have any real friends, didn't know how to change that, wasn't even sure she wanted to. I had the same experience every day at school, sitting in class surrounded by people who seemed to speak and exist just behind some invisible barrier I couldn't breach. And although some days I would have given anything to break through it, other days I wasn't really sure I wanted to. Even now, all these years later, I still don't know whether I kept my distance from people because I wanted to, or because I felt there was no choice; whether it would have been better to make the effort it seemed I needed to make rather than do what I did and convince myself I didn't really care either way. I felt like Pluto or some other distant planet, so far from it all that I was hardly there, and far enough that I could watch it all without being watched in turn. Perhaps Clara was like Pluto too, though much later, I would come to understand that she was really more like the moon. When there was nothing to hold her back, when she could exist at her brightest, she seemed to make the whole world gleam. But there was another side to her that she never let people see, a strange sadness she seemed always to carry with her, hidden away. You could only tell that it was there because sometimes its shadow would spill over into her light.

But I didn't know any of that back then. That day on Old Mrs Dickie's burgundy couch, Clara was all light. We talked for hours – about our favourite teachers and our least favourite books, and about what might happen in the new season of *Breakers*, the TV show every teenager in the country had been obsessed with for the past year. When one of us paused to sip on the lemonade her grandma had made for us, the other took over. We only stopped when Old Mrs Dickie came back inside from her gardening and asked if I would like to stay for dinner. I was polite enough to know this meant I should probably go home. In the hallway, Clara asked me if I'd like to come back the next day; we could have a picnic in the back garden if I wanted to. I told her that sounded wonderful.

*

Everything I saw as I cycled back home that day made me laugh. Even the extreme heat seemed funny, precisely because it was so unusually intense. Whenever my bare skin accidentally brushed against the metal frame of the bike, there was a sting like being pinched by a small child with tiny fingers. But it wasn't annoying; it was hilarious. The wilting shrubs in people's dried-up gardens seemed alive; I could make out faces in the leaves, like cartoon characters. The two old ladies who lived in the second-biggest house on our street had left their windows open, vainly hoping for a breeze. They were sitting in their living room, inexplicably wearing shower caps. Perhaps they were worried that the wet heat would curl their hair, but the shower caps made their heads look like cauliflowers. The image made me laugh; tomorrow I would tell Clara about it and make her laugh too.

4

WHEN I woke up the next day, I was excited before I could even remember why. I blinked at the ceiling, already awash with sunlight pooling in through the window. By the time I got dressed and went downstairs, my mother was already gone. I had long since been old enough that she could go out to work even when I was home for the summer holidays. Her job was to look after other people's kids – mostly very young children whose parents both worked full-time. By all accounts my mother loved other people's children. She was very good with them. They responded to her instructions, they trusted and understood her, and she certainly understood them. She couldn't really understand me, though;

every now and then she would ask me why I was so quiet, and one time I overheard her on the phone to my aunt, telling her she wished I could be more like other kids. 'I know teenagers can be like this sometimes, but this is too much. I never know what she's thinking. All she does is read. She doesn't even have any friends.'

Perhaps that was why the excitement I had woken up with wore off so quickly and was replaced, halfway down the road to Old Mrs Dickie's house, with a less pleasant feeling of apprehension. What if Clara hadn't actually meant it when she'd said to come and visit her again? What if she was just being nice? What if we found we had nothing left to talk about? Had Old Mrs Dickie's house been a little further away, I might have turned around and gone back home, but by the time that possibility had even occurred to me, it was already too late. I knocked on the door and a few moments later, Old Mrs Dickie opened it. 'Hello, dear. Come on through; Clara's out in the garden.'

Unlike the rest of Old Mrs Dickie's house, which was ordinary in every way, her back garden was unusually vast. It bordered to the right on a narrow, muddy creek, beyond which a low wire fence and an uneven row of trees and bushes marked the edge of what must have been someone else's backyard. To the left was the other neighbour's garden, but where that garden ended, backing into a row of mulberry trees, Old Mrs Dickie's continued all the way down to a straggly patch of woodland known locally as the thicket. When we were little and school was out, we would often dare each other to cut through the thicket from the other end and see how close we could get to Old Mrs Dickie before she spotted us. We would crouch low among the bushes, deaf to the rustling we were making, and peer at her through the treeline as she tended to her roses or watered her lemon tree. We would emerge from the thicket with loping, comically exaggerated strides, unable to stifle our giggles, yet still Old Mrs Dickie wouldn't turn. Then, when we were only a few feet away, she would suddenly drop what she was doing and whip her head around, mouth twisted into a grimace, eyes wide open under the brim of her green sun hat, and we would scramble back to the safety of the thicket, squealing in terrified delight. We stopped playing the game when we got older and realized that Old Mrs Dickie must have been able to hear us coming well before we reached the edge of her garden, and was only pretending not to see us. But there were always other, younger neighbourhood children to continue the tradition.

Now I was approaching the thicket from the other side. The sun was almost blinding, and at first I couldn't see Clara. But then she called my name from under a tree by the creek, and I walked over to her. She was wearing a white T-shirt which somehow appeared even whiter in the shade. Everything around her was green, including the blanket she was sitting on. When I was very little, I used to have a picture book called *Life in the Forest*, and in that picture book there was a drawing called *The Woodland Nymph*. I hadn't thought about that drawing in years, but I remembered it now.

'I was afraid you wouldn't come,' she said, then looked away as if she wished she hadn't said that. Any doubts I still had as to whether it had been a good idea to take her up on her invitation vanished instantly.

I sat down beside her, cross-legged. Clara had never heard of *Life in the Forest*, but we quickly discovered that we had both been obsessed with the same series of books about the space pilot Nadia, who captained a battered old rocket ship called the SS *Vela*. Its only crew members were an anthropomorphic cat named Lynx and a young woman called Rosa, an orphan whom Nadia had met on one of her adventures and rescued from an uncertain future. Nadia and her crew got into all sorts of scrapes. They were perpetually having to make emergency landings because the *Vela* was such an old jalopy (this was the word the author used; neither of us was quite sure how it was pronounced as we'd never heard it spoken aloud), and often the inhabitants of the planets they landed upon were suspicious of these newcomers, if not openly hostile. But they were invariably won over by Nadia, who was so charming, so charismatic and so clever that it was impossible not to love her. In fact, both Clara and I suspected that Rosa was probably in love with Nadia. It was never made explicit, nor was there any other trace of romance in these books, which were designed for young readers more interested in aliens and intergalactic travel. But both of us could discern something in Rosa's single-minded devotion to Nadia, in the way she wouldn't let anyone say a word against her – not even Lynx, not even as a joke – that told us that she didn't just admire Nadia, wasn't just grateful to her for rescuing her from the desert planet she'd been born and orphaned on, but that she loved her, loved her with all her heart and wanted nothing but to spend the rest of her life by her side. Whenever Nadia did something particularly heroic, pulled off an especially brilliant feat to aid the bedraggled inhabitants of the latest planet the *Vela* had landed upon, Rosa would glow with pride. And when Nadia was mobbed by grateful well-wishers hoping to catch one last glimpse of her before she hopped jauntily back into her patched-up vessel, Rosa would step in to shield her beloved captain from the excesses of collective euphoria, her actions signalling to all those present that she was Nadia's right-hand woman, her protector, her most loyal confidante.

Clara told me that sometimes, when she had trouble falling asleep, she would make up Nadia adventures in her head. Like the books themselves, her versions followed a similar trajectory every time. The *Vela* would crash-land onto a planet that happened to be in some kind of trouble. While they waited for spare parts to fix the *Vela*'s hydrogen reactor or its oxygen monitor or its waste-filtering system, Nadia, Rosa and Lynx would get to know the planet and its people, gain their trust and provide some small but crucial assistance to help them fix whatever trouble they were in. Yet in Clara's night-time imaginings, the crew's adventures were more violent, more treacherous, more tragic than in the books. She would imagine Nadia mortally wounded while helping to fight off evil intergalactic raiders or rescuing people trapped under the rubble of an asteroid strike, and she would lull herself to sleep with the silent image of the dead hero Nadia, mourned and beloved by all, cradled in Rosa's arms.

'Is that weird?' she asked, looking a little unsure.

I didn't think so. One evening when I was little, I had accidentally watched a film I was far too young for, a bloody medieval epic in which a brave warrior led a rebellion against a tyrannical baron. Near the end of the film the hero was wounded by an arrow in his side, and his most trusted lieutenants carried him away on horseback to a secluded cave. His wife was already there when they arrived, having received the news from a messenger. When she saw her fallen, bleeding husband, she let out a strangled cry, but quickly pulled herself together, rushing to his side and helping him off the horse. In the cave, she lay him down on a bed of straw, then carefully removed his armour and began tending to his many wounds, stitching them up herself and wiping the blood off with a wet rag. Throughout this whole ordeal, the warrior barely made a sound – only the occasional sharp intake of breath revealing the pain he was in – and once the stitching was done and his wife had wrapped makeshift bandages around his ribs, he brought his right hand to the side of her face. He caressed her lips with his thumb and pulled her in for a kiss, the camera panning to a small fire flickering in the background and lingering there for several seconds before the film moved on to the following scene.

My memory of what happened next in the film was hazy, though I was fairly sure the warrior recovered from his wounds and led his people to liberty. Yet I remembered that scene in the cave so vividly that years later, I would still find myself thinking about it from time to time. It was strangely comforting, like picking at a spot or pressing a fingernail into a mosquito bite. But I never got to the part where the hero emerged from the cave, healed and ready to return to the rebellion. My daydreams would linger in the cave, on the way his wife had wiped the blood off as he gritted his teeth in pain, on her tears falling across his face as they kissed.

I told Clara about the film and how I still thought about my favourite cave scene, and she listened closely and quietly, nodding in understanding. When I was done she smiled, then let herself fall backwards onto the blanket, one arm by her side and the other stretched out to her right. Her hand reached just beyond the edge of the fabric; she tore out a blade of grass and started winding and unwinding it around her index finger. I looked at her face and found that she was looking at me as if she were about to say something. But she didn't, so I spoke instead.

'How come we've never seen you here before?'

She turned her gaze towards the sky and closed her eyes. Her right hand stilled, the blade of grass now loose around her finger. I felt a heat creeping up my face.

'My mum and my grandma don't really talk anymore,' she said eventually. She opened her eyes again but kept them fixed on the canopy above our heads. It looked like she was holding her breath.

'Sorry. I didn't mean to pry.'

'That's okay. It's just that I'm not supposed to talk about it. It's meant to be a family secret. Please don't tell anyone.'

'Of course not.'

We fell silent. Clara was looking up at the trees again, the palm of her right hand skimming over the grass. I could feel the back of my T-shirt clinging to my skin, and sweat gathering on my temples and at the nape of my neck. I tilted my head back and the sweat trickled into the collar of my T-shirt. I saw a bird fly quickly and quietly across the gap between two adjacent trees. It was so humid that the air above our heads was distorted, as if we were looking through a thick pane of glass, and the leaves on the trees seeped into one another like green jelly. I kicked my shoes off and lay on my back next to Clara, but further down the blanket, so that my head was level with her shoulders and my feet were on the grass. The blanket rubbed against my calves and the backs of my knees, but not in an unpleasant way. I was as contented as I would have been on my own rocking chair; the only difference was that if I listened carefully, I could hear the faint sound of Clara breathing next to me. In the heat and the green haze that seemed to surround us both like a physical presence, I felt intensely awake.

*

That night, I couldn't sleep. It was too hot, and I kept thinking about Clara's family secret, the mysterious rift between her mother and her mother's mother. She hadn't explained what had caused it, and I hadn't asked, but it must have been something significant. Perhaps one day they would have a big emotional reconciliation, like in the movies, but as I had never met Clara's mother and didn't know what she looked like, I found the scene difficult to picture. Instead, my thoughts kept drifting to my own mother, whom I hardly saw or spoke to anymore, even though we lived in the same house. She had once again fallen asleep on the couch after dinner.

An awful prickly heat began to spread through my chest and shoulders, keeping me pinned to the bed so that I felt I couldn't move even if I wanted to. I closed my eyes but I kept seeing Clara's sad, mysterious expression, her faceless mother, my own silent mother. The heavy, pinning heat grew stronger, until I felt as if I might sink into the mattress. I recognized this sensation from the days and months after my father had left, and it was terrifying to think I might have to spend the whole night feeling that way. So I started thinking about Nadia instead. I imagined that she and Lynx and Rosa had joined a group of fighters from a tiny fringe planet in the outer galaxies on a mission to rescue a group of children with extremely rare telekinetic abilities from a gang of militias who had abducted them and taken them away to a neighbouring planet. The mission was a success, the children were rescued, the militias scattered into the galactic night. But in that hour of joyful, exuberant triumph, nobody realized that Nadia had been wounded – not even Nadia herself. Only once they had returned to the private quarters their hosts had provided them with did Nadia remove her body armour, revealing a deep bleeding gash in her abdomen. The next moment, she collapsed onto her camp bed and it was clear that she was going to die. Rosa sobbed at her bedside, desperate with grief. Lynx fetched a doctor who managed to stem the bleeding enough to give Nadia a few more minutes, but the kind of advanced medical technology that might have saved her life was not available on this isolated planet, and in any case it was probably too late for it now.

The doctor left the room, shaking his head sombrely. Lynx wept into his paws as he and Nadia exchanged a final farewell, then he too padded out so that Rosa and Nadia might have a moment alone. Rosa clung to Nadia, saying over and over again, 'Don't leave me, please don't leave me,' kissing Nadia's eyes, her forehead, her shoulder, her hair, as Nadia also wept and whispered to Rosa how scared she was, how sorry she was, and how much she loved her.

Rosa, Nadia and Lynx were hiding behind a charging pylon on the edge of the square. The night sky was tinged with red and orange and smelled of the chemical fires that had been raging all day across this beleaguered town. The bandits responsible for the damage were loitering in the square where they had landed their spaceship, firing their laser pistols into the sky for fun, revelling in the chaos and sorting their loot. Their leader, the notorious Goondock, stood among them, supervising the proceedings with a satisfied sneer.

Nadia was furious. 'We can't let them carry on like this, acting like they own the place.'

'But there's too many of them, captain,' said Lynx. 'How are we going to take them on?'

'We won't do it alone. The people of this town want to fight back; they just don't know how. Look up – see those people at the windows? They're ready; they just need someone to lead them.'

She was right. All around the square, people were standing at their windows, watching the galactic gangsters who had commandeered their market square. Even in the darkness of night you could see how angry they were. This was the sixth time in four seasons that Goondock and his crew had raided their town. They had appealed to the capital for protection, but the capital itself was constantly under threat from bandits and couldn't do much to help. It was not an unusual situation for an outer planet to be in, but even so, when Nadia and her crew had landed here for emergency repairs, they had not expected to find themselves in the midst of such a crisis. How were they going to fix this?

Rosa closed her eyes and took three deep breaths. She was not as confident as Nadia, not as strong or dexterous as Lynx, but this was what she was good at: planning. She could plan for any contingency and she could always work out how to make the best of an impossible situation. It was what she had been doing all her life; it was how she had survived her childhood. When she opened her eyes again, she knew exactly what to do.

A triumphant roar rose from the townspeople of Renania as they watched the bandits' spaceship take off in humiliating retreat, carrying only Goondock and the handful of his followers who had managed to scramble onto the ship with him. The remaining bandits sat bundled together on one side of the square, hands and feet tied up, gazing glumly at the loot they had hoped to take with them. The town's four human medics had arrived to treat those with superficial wounds, while a few people with more serious injuries – including a couple of the bandits – were hovered to the nearest RoboClinic. The little local boy whom Rosa had tasked with spreading word that the crew of the SS Vela *was here to help was now sitting on his father's shoulders, people reaching up to shake his hand and pat him on the back as he told the story of how he had crept through the night with his secret message. Meanwhile, Lynx was talking to the town elders and handing out the laser pistols that had been confiscated from the bandits. They were older models, but they would be good enough to help the town defend itself should Goondock or any other space bandit choose to return.*

Rosa and Nadia sat side by side on a bench on the edge of the square, where every now and then someone would approach them to thank them for their help. A local plumber who had heard about the Vela*'s broken quark binder offered her services for free; a man who ran a tavern nearby brought them food; and an old woman whose home had been destroyed by the* *bandits came up to kiss their foreheads. But the festive mood barely registered with Rosa and Nadia. The adrenaline from the fight had worn off, and all they could think of now was how easily things could have gone wrong, how easily someone could have ended up dead. In the distance, plumes of black smoke rose up to the sky, a visible reminder of what the town had endured and what it might well soon face again.*

Rosa looked at Nadia and saw in her face the same numb exhaustion she herself was feeling.

'That was close,' she said.

Nadia nodded, glassy-eyed.

'It's tough coming to these outer planets,' she said. 'It makes you wonder. The people who live here, they are ordinary people, they are not so different from us. But they have all of this to contend with. We just so happened to be here to help this time, but soon we'll be gone again. What then?'

A great wave of sorrow swelled inside Rosa. She could hardly breathe from it. All of a sudden she was back in New Saturn, the home she had left behind and would probably never see again. But New Saturn had not left her: she thought about it every day, of its barren plains, of its people hardened by the elements, of her parents whose faces she only remembered thanks to the repros she carried in her pocket. Life on New Saturn had not been so different from life here on this unfortunate planet, but after Rosa's parents had died, it had become a struggle just to exist. Rosa would go to bed in the cold, empty house wondering how she was going to survive another day. What would her life have been like now if Nadia and Lynx had never landed on New Saturn on their way to Ibadan? Or if Rosa hadn't happened to be there when they'd got lost in the web-like streets of the shipmongers' quarter? And what about all the people who still lived and struggled on in New Saturn, the neighbours who had tried to help Rosa when they could, the old man who sold banana stew from a cart at the end of the road and always gave Rosa a discount, the medic who had healed her when she had broken her wrist and the RoboClinic wouldn't take her unless she could pay in advance?

One by one the tears began to fall. Rosa couldn't stop them. They came like a flood.

'Rosa? Rosa, why are you crying? What is it, what's wrong?'

'This place …' she began, but it was hard to find the right words. She tried again. 'This place … This is what it was like, back home.'

Nadia had asked her so many times about New Saturn, what life had been like for her, how she had survived there as an orphan. But Rosa hadn't told her much: some part of her had always been afraid that talking about her past might tarnish the life she was living now. Rosa was not a mere passenger on the Vela. *Nadia and Lynx relied on her. They trusted her judgement. Nadia treated her like an equal, had done so since the day they'd met. She did not want that to change. She did not want Nadia to feel sorry for her. Even now, two Earth Years after they had left New Saturn together, Rosa was afraid that she might lose what she still couldn't quite believe she had found.*

'What do you mean? What do you mean, Rosa? Say something, please,' Nadia pleaded.

But Rosa just shook her head. She couldn't push past the silence inside her. When she felt Nadia's arm come around her shoulders, she turned her face into Nadia's shoulder and sobbed.

5

In the weeks that followed, Clara and I saw each other every day. We spent every moment together, reading side by side in whatever patch of shade we managed to snatch from the overbearing heat; splashing about in the creek; and watching a terrible cooking show presented by a greasy-haired chef who kept referring to the ingredients as his 'friends' and whose signature move was to 'garnish' every dish with inexplicable quantities of extra virgin olive oil. We had become instantly, almost comically inseparable. If anyone happened to spot us apart, they would ask where our shadow had gone, and even my mother had noticed that something was different: at dinner times, I was quieter than I had ever been, deflated and distracted by an unfamiliar longing, and in the mornings I'd wake up much earlier than I used to, in time to have breakfast with her before running outside to grab my bike and cycle over to see Clara. I told her about my new friend over breakfast one day when she finally asked me where it was that I kept running away to. She smiled at me then with a warmth in her eyes that I hadn't seen in a long time. 'She sounds lovely. You should invite her for dinner some time. I'd love to meet her,' she said, laying her hand gently on my wrist. I looked down at my plate, feeling embarrassed and awkward but also weirdly happy, and told her I would think about it.

One of our other favourite activities was to go cycling around town, Clara on a battered old bike she had borrowed from one of her grandmother's neighbours. We would roam around for hours, hopping from one shop awning to another in search of whatever shade the town had to offer, and eating more ice cream than I would have ever thought possible – an ice cream every hour, on the hour, until it became part of the language we used between us to measure time and temperature. This was but one part of the secret code we soon developed for our forays into town. People we deemed boring or ordinary, we called 'oblongs', while those we suspected of having secretly eventful lives were 'wobblies'.

I would struggle now to identify the criteria through which we reached these kinds of conclusions; it must have had something to do with the kinds of shoes people wore and how they styled their hair, but I am sure there were less tangible measures too. For people our own age, though, we had no code. Instead, we would take care to avoid them, watching them from behind a pillar or a tree until they were at a safe distance, and if I knew who they were – as I sometimes did, especially if they happened to go to my school – I would give Clara potted histories of their lives so far. If I didn't know them, we'd make their stories up together.

One day we saw two of the boys I used to roam around with when I was younger. One of them still looked as scrawny as he had back then, only much taller now and with longer hair. The other had grown to be quite good-looking. I'd already noticed this the previous summer, and it was even more evident this year, though I remember registering the fact with a certain kind of scientific detachment, like a botanist observing an unfamiliar specimen. They were walking in our direction on the pavement across the street, but I had no idea whether they remembered me, and the last thing I wanted was to find out. I pulled Clara towards me so that we were hidden behind a tree that was probably older than all four of us put together. She looked surprised for a second and nearly dropped her ice cream, but when she saw me looking at the two boys across the road, she understood immediately. I felt relieved and grateful. We watched them walking down the pavement, leaning our backs against the tree trunk and trying to look casual. 'So, who were they, then?' she asked me once they were well out of earshot. I explained about the swimming pool, the phone call, the tragic wasted swimsuit. She looked so outraged that it made the whole thing seem funny, and I felt none of the residual embarrassment I normally did whenever something reminded me of that incident. At Clara's suggestion, we finished our ice creams – probably our third or fourth of the day – and cycled slowly towards the public swimming pool, a squat, mud-brown building with thick hedges all around so that the pool itself was completely hidden from view. We sat on a bench outside in the shade of the building and spent the rest of the afternoon watching people come and go, staring haughtily at anyone who happened to be roughly our age, making faces at the younger kids, rolling our eyes at the frazzled, apprehensive, heat-stricken parents who came to drop them off or collect them. We only left because we'd forgotten to bring water and wanted more ice cream. As we made our way back towards the centre of town, wheeling our bicycles along and elaborating on all the backstories we had invented for the people we had seen that day, I remember thinking that if those two boys from earlier were to walk past us again, this time I wouldn't hide behind a tree, but I would link my arm with Clara's and laugh extra loudly to make sure they saw and heard me.

*

Every few days we met up with Joe. We would go to his house to eat home-made ice cream and to play with Sheba, who had taken to Clara immediately – as she did with all newcomers – and refused to let her out of her sight. When we were with Joe, we became a slightly different version of ourselves. We spoke more casually, we were never serious, we teased each other constantly. But whenever he went inside for something to eat, or even when his back was turned for a moment, we would fall back into our own secret ways, our language of knowing smiles and silent communion. We had fun with Joe, but always, after we said goodbye and promised Sheba we'd see her again soon, Clara and I would spend whatever time we had left before we had to go home for dinner talking through every moment of the day, carving each other's thoughts open as if to consolidate our shared view of reality.

At night, before we went to sleep, we would write each other notes so that we could swap them the next day and catch up on what we had missed. No event was too minor, no detail superfluous. Anything we didn't experience together was worth recording, ready to be pored over the next day. It was like talking into a mirror, except the reflection wasn't your own, and it talked back, laughing in all the right places and commiserating on all the right mishaps. *Grandma told me about her first boyfriend today – very hilarious,* she wrote one time. The full story was three pages long, full of doodles and crossings-out and tiny, terrible drawings of stick figures in top hats. When I read it the next day, she re-enacted all the best parts for me, doing an uncanny impression of Old Mrs Dickie – though she would have been young, then – hopping onto the back of this guy's dirty motorbike every Thursday evening, because that was the day she finished work early. It was unclear what he did for a living, except for being *a full-time lovable rogue*. One night, on their *three-month anniversary* (Clara had dotted the 'i' in anniversary with a heart), he brought her a jar of pickles as a gift. It bore no label and the pickling juices were so murky that she couldn't even tell what vegetable it was supposed to be. She *strongly suspected* the pickle was home-made, which was all the more reason never to open the jar. Clara then launched into some invented pickling instructions, and we laughed so hard – over nothing at all, really – that I felt dizzy afterwards.

My own night-time musings to Clara heavily featured my latest obsession: a book about optical illusions, which I had found on a shelf in the kitchen, mysteriously wedged between two cookbooks. One day I brought it with me so I could show it to her. There were dots spiralling on a stationary page, never-ending staircases, two identical orange squares that looked different colours depending on the backgrounds they were printed on, and many more things of that sort that I have mostly forgotten now. I loved this book because it was so clearly meant for kids in a way that, at sixteen, I was already old enough to find nostalgic: the type was huge, the illustrations cartoonish, the explanations so simplified as to be almost misleading. It reminded me of another book of this sort that I had been fascinated with a few years before, also clearly designed for children. It had an ugly pea-green cover, and inside, the paper was glossy and smelled like glue. The title – *The World's Greatest Unsolved Mysteries: A Guide for Inquiring Minds* – had always made me feel so clever and grown up. There was a chapter on the lost city of Atlantis, a whole section on UFOs, even a particularly spooky passage on spontaneous combustion, which I had completely forgotten until I started telling Clara about it and we laughed in delighted horror at the idea of sitting in an armchair one moment and bursting into flames the next. But the chapter that had impressed itself upon me most vividly was the one about the Bermuda Triangle. I told Clara of how I'd had nightmares about it for months, where I would be on a plane – never a boat, somehow – that strayed over the edge of the triangle and blinked itself out of existence. I would wake up terrified and find it hard to go back to sleep afterwards. I had told my parents about it one morning, who, to their credit, didn't laugh, but attempted instead to reassure me, pointing out that the chances of my ever being on a plane flying over the Bermuda Triangle were very slim indeed, and perhaps this was not quite the kind of danger I needed to worry about. I couldn't remember if their attempt at reassurance had worked – though, as Clara pointed out, it must have done some good, given that I was laughing about it now.

'I watched a documentary about tornadoes once when I was little,' she told me. 'After that, I was so scared of natural disasters that I couldn't sleep. It didn't even have to be tornadoes – it could be floods, it could be earthquakes, or a meteor falling from the sky. One time, it was a dinosaur invasion.' We laughed a little at this, and she looked so sweet and sheepish that I almost gave her a hug. The dreams, she said, were always the same – 'some kind of awful destruction approaching, I can see it in the distance, I can see which way it's going, and I have to make sure I get away, but my parents have disappeared and I am so worried about them, I have no idea what to do, so I start to panic – and then I'd wake up. I would always be relieved it was a dream, but there was also this feeling that if only I'd stayed asleep a little longer, I would have maybe figured out what to do, how to make it to safety, and then I wouldn't be so scared anymore.'

'So you basically wanted the nightmare to continue?'

She lowered her eyes and started tracing the pattern on the blanket with the edge of her thumbnail. Then she looked up again, her lips pursed in concentration.

'I guess I wanted to solve it. So that I could be prepared if it happened in real life,' she said, her eyes gleaming with the satisfaction of having figured something out. She turned to look at a bird that had just flown past us, and I thought to myself that she was surely the most interesting person I had ever met.

6

In later years I often found myself wondering what it was that had drawn me to Clara so intensely. Of course I had been lonely, but that explained only part of it. It explained why I felt grateful for her company, relieved to be sought out, to be selected in this way. But it did not explain how easy and comfortable it was to be around her, nor the sense of anticipation with which I went to bed every night, knowing that as soon as I woke up, I would have a whole other day with her to look forward to.

I'd had a 'best friend' once before – a girl at school a couple of years before I met Clara. We had been thrown together by the fact of our respective isolation, the lack of other company to keep. But otherwise we had little in common; we liked each other and got along well enough, but we also thought in different ways and cared about different things. She was steelier than I was and more independent. Neither of us felt inclined to see the other outside of school hours, and eventually we drifted apart as casually as we had come together. I still saw her around in school sometimes. She had not replaced me with anyone else, and appeared to be fairly content with her lot. In that respect, perhaps, we were more similar than in any other.

As a child, I had mostly played with stuffed animals. They were the only toys I ever asked for. I used to make up all kinds of adventures for them: mountain rescues, polar expeditions, battles between good and evil across my bedroom floor. There were epic friendships, emotional confrontations, deathbed scenes, sporting competitions. Though I tried to be fair and give them all a chance to be the hero, I had favourites – in particular a lion cub my parents had bought me at the luna park, and whom I had unimaginatively named Leo. At night I would always bring at least three or four of my stuffed toys into bed with me, but while most of them experienced this privilege on rotation, Leo's place by my pillow was guaranteed.

My interest in crafting complex storylines for my

stuffed animals to re-enact naturally waned as I grew up, but the toys remained in my room, arranged in a semicircle on my chest of drawers as a sweet, dusty reminder of childhood games. The sole exception was Leo, who sat contentedly on my bedside table. At school one day, many years before the summer I met Clara, we were waiting in class for a substitute teacher to arrive: everyone was talking, and I remember making an immense effort to be involved and say something that they would find interesting. I don't know why, but I decided to tell the two girls sitting nearest to me about Leo. As soon as I did, they started laughing at me. I had not been prepared for that, and couldn't make sense of it, for I was sure that both of them must have had their own versions of Leo too, and would have felt awful if people had laughed at them for it. I spent so much time every day feeling just slightly bored and out of kilter with everyone around me and now, once again, I seemed to have misjudged something. I remember feeling a deep sense of unbelonging, but most of all, fury. I turned away, taking out my pencil case and notebook and deciding then and there that I would never forgive them and never speak to them again. It reminded me of the time my mother had fallen out with one of her oldest friends. I never found out exactly why; she just stopped seeing her or mentioning her, so suddenly that it was as though this woman had never existed in the first place. I'd been quite young when this happened, so I don't think it had really registered at the time as a particularly noteworthy event, but I understood the emotion behind it now. Those girls had never really been my friends, so the sting of it was not as sharp for me. But I remember thinking very clearly that they had wronged me, and so I was better off without them.

When I told Clara about Leo, she started laughing too, but somehow I knew that she wasn't making fun of me. She listened to my self-consciously long-winded explanations of how I'd got him and how long I'd had him for, how the texture of his fur changed every time my mother put him in the washing machine, how he'd lost an eye once and my mum had taught me how to sew it back on. Then she told me about a Lego set she had been gifted for her birthday one year, in which one of the Lego figurines wore sunglasses and a black cape. Of all her childhood toys, this tiny piece of plastic, this Lego man, was the one she had played with the most. 'I used to talk to him, and in my head he would reply to me. Obviously I knew it wasn't real, but I had so much fun with him. I thought he was so *handsome*! Can you believe it?' she said, now laughing at herself. 'He lives on my bedside table too, you know.'

'I also think Leo is very handsome,' I told her, hiding

my face in my hands. 'I still talk to him sometimes when I can't sleep.'

I peered through my fingers to find her grinning at me. 'We must introduce them to each other. Leo and Mr Lego-Man!' she said.

We burst out laughing.

It is a rare and precious feeling to be able to share something with another person, something small and trivial or quite important, and to be held in their mind and understood in their heart, and feel not quite so alone, not quite so bewildered anymore. In that respect, talking to Clara was almost like talking to myself. It did not seem necessary to filter any of my thoughts when I was with her, a feeling I was so entirely unaccustomed to that I would sometimes stop abruptly, afraid that I'd said something too strange, too dull, or that was surely only of interest to me. But then she would look up from the daisy chain she was making or from the spider she was busy corralling off the edge of the picnic blanket and peer at me with just the hint of a frown, as if to say *Well? Why did you stop there?* And so it was that I found myself telling Clara about things I had hardly yet told myself: that sometimes I pretended I enjoyed spending time by myself more than I actually did; that I wished we had more money so we could go on holiday again like we used to do; that it was probably wrong of my father to leave us the way he had. This was *his* home town, after all; he didn't have to move so far away. He could have stayed closer to us. He could have stayed closer to me.

'After my father left, I was convinced for a very long time that it must have been because of something I'd done. Or maybe even something I'd forgotten to do,' I started telling her one day as we hacked our way through the thicket to gather leaves for a flower arrangement her grandmother had asked us to help with. I had been like a child out of the movies, back then – blaming myself for my parents being unhappy with each other even though they must have told me a thousand times that it had nothing to do with me. But it had taken me ages to believe it, and when I finally did, I became really angry, because if it wasn't my fault, then it followed that it must be theirs. 'It's been nearly three years now since they separated,' I said to Clara, 'but sometimes I still feel so angry that I refuse to speak to my dad when he calls. But I guess being angry at him or at my mum is better than being angry at myself?'

I stopped there, surprised at the outpouring of words that I had produced on a subject I never, ever spoke about, except sometimes to myself in quiet conversations in my own head which never really went anywhere and that, if I wasn't careful and let them go on for too long, would leave me with a sick feeling in my stomach and a sense of precarious control over my arms and legs. But just as it was unimaginable that I should speak of these feelings with anyone other than Clara, it was equally unimaginable not to speak of them with her. It was like a compulsion. She had to know everything there was to know about me, every strange little thought and every weird little dream I had ever had. The instinct for self-preservation that usually loomed so large over every other aspect of my life seemed non-existent – unnecessary, even – where Clara was concerned. She understood me completely.

Clara told me stories too. Her mother, she said, was famously beautiful. That was the exact phrase she used. She also had what were known in the family as 'moods'. It was sometimes implied that the two things – her beauty and these 'moods' – were somehow correlated, as if the former inevitably caused the latter. Clara and I had both read enough novels to know that this manner of thinking about women and their moods was not at all original. On the other hand, it seemed clear to us, in the certainty of our youthful convictions, that there was a connection between the cadence of her mother's periodic bouts of anguish and that of Clara's father's business trips – a connection so clear and obvious that it was not such a great leap to deduce that the cause of these so-called moods her mother was known for almost as much as she was for her beauty lay not in some mysterious link between beauty and melancholy, but in the more banal notion that when her husband was away, Clara's mother was lonely. So she couldn't help it, Clara continued, but she often felt angry at her father for being gone for work so often, sometimes for weeks at a stretch. When he was home, Clara and her mother would feast on him – I vividly remember her using that word because it sounded so strange in that context, and yet so perfectly clear. When he was home, Clara felt like a little girl again. We were sitting in the shade by the creek in Old Mrs Dickie's garden one afternoon, our feet dangling in the water, when she told me she had once caught herself literally tugging at her father's shirtsleeve to try to get his attention. Her mother and her father had both laughed at her – good-naturedly, of course, Clara knew that much, but nonetheless she had felt so mortified that she'd fled to her room so they wouldn't see her crying. It had taken her several minutes to compose herself, for the redness to fade from her cheeks, and when she'd gone back downstairs they'd obviously forgotten the whole incident and she'd had to pretend it hadn't happened at all.

'Do you think it was stupid to get so worked up about it?' she asked me, turning her face away from mine.

'No,' I said, a stinging heat creeping up and across the bridge of my nose. 'It was stupid of them to laugh at you.' I wasn't sure why, but it reminded me of something I'd done when I was little, though old enough to know exactly what I was doing, and definitely old enough to know better. It was back when my parents were still together, and well before that time, towards the end, when they tried to stay together even though neither seemed particularly happy to be doing so. They had organized a small dinner party at our house, inviting two other couples they had befriended on a package holiday we'd been on the summer before. These two couples also had kids, and although their children were a little older than I was, they'd been kind to me during that holiday and included me in their games, making sure to let me win sometimes and denying that they'd done so on purpose even when it was obvious. But the children didn't come to our house that night; only their parents. I remember Mum and Dad had sat me between them, and for a whole heady hour I had been treated almost like a grown-up, involved in the conversation and asked my opinions of whatever they were discussing. I had sensed something unusual in their manner – what I now recognize as the well-meaning, indulgent amusement that adults can derive from the company and conversation of serious, well-behaved children. But although those are the kind of children who are most likely to recognize and maybe even resent that soft edge of benevolent condescension, they are also the same children who will most enjoy, and sometimes crave, the feeling of being treated a little differently from how other kids their age might be. When they eventually ran out of questions to ask me and topics that could possibly interest me – which was around the time my mother brought in the ice cream and fruit she had decided to serve for dessert – I felt as if I'd suddenly become invisible. I slid off my chair with my bowl of ice cream and went to sit on the blue-and-white-striped rug in front of the television, where I usually played with my airport set or watched cartoons in the early morning. I looked at my parents and the other adults to see if they would notice that I'd left the table, but they didn't seem to. I turned my back to them, facing the black TV screen, the bowl of ice cream balanced on my lap. Soon the ice cream began to melt; I wasn't eating it fast enough and now it had turned into brown sludge with a few white lumps floating in it, because for some reason the vanilla ice cream was melting more slowly than the chocolate. I turned around to look at my parents again but I could see only the backs of their heads. I lifted the bowl of melted ice cream from my lap and tipped it onto the carpet.

The clinking of the spoon as it fell out of the bowl must have attracted my parents' attention. 'Are you all right there, darling?' I heard my mother say. I looked around over my shoulder again and saw the moment she noticed the spill on the rug – a flash of annoyance, rapidly mastered, a hint of weariness. My father turned around and saw the mess too; he put his hand on the back of her chair as if to say *I'll handle it*, then pushed his chair back so that he could stand, all the while laughing at a story someone else had just been telling. He rolled his napkin into a cylinder and dipped one end into his glass of water, then came over to where I was still sitting, staring helplessly at the upturned bowl and the oozing stain. He crouched down and smiled. 'Let's clean this up, shall we? Then I'll get you some more.'

He wiped the spoon clean, then used it to scoop up as much of the melted ice cream as he could, before starting to rub at the stain with the wet napkin. He asked me to go into the kitchen to fetch a clean rag and some dishwashing liquid. I must have looked upset when I came back, because when he saw me standing there, watching him clean up the mess I had made, he said: 'There's no reason to get upset, peanut; it's not like you did it on purpose!'

There was so much certainty in his voice that of course I couldn't tell him I'd done exactly that. I'd begun to feel guilty from the moment I had tipped the bowl over, and now I felt even worse; but at the same time I had managed to get what I wanted, even if it was only temporarily. My mum came over on her way back from the kitchen, where she'd gone to get me a fresh bowl; she took my hand and led me back to the table, then gave me another scoop each of the chocolate and vanilla and a spoonful of fruit. I ate the fruit without complaint and finished the ice cream before it could melt.

I had never told anyone that story before; in fact I'd almost forgotten it had ever happened. But it seemed natural to tell Clara then. She listened carefully, and when I was done, she scooted up to me and hugged me, her arms hot and sticky across my shoulders, her face turned away so that the top of her head nestled in the crook of my neck.

7

One Thursday morning, about halfway through the summer, the travelling theatre came to town. This was not necessarily an annual occurrence, and in a place where hardly anything new ever happened, its arrival was always greeted with great excitement, bordering at times on mass hysteria. During their brief and irregular forays into our town, the members of the travelling theatre would find themselves thrust into the centre of a collective worship, their talents magnified, their private lives and predilections the object of endless speculation. Yet although their every move was tracked and commented upon, they were also kept at arm's length, as if they belonged to another category of human that it wouldn't quite do to approach. The prevailing consensus was that they were fascinating creatures, but that they must not be disturbed, lest their preparations for the evening's performance should be disrupted.

Three years ago – the last time they had come through our town – they had staged a production of *Antigone*, a play I had never heard of before. They had not attempted to adapt it for a modern audience, going instead to great lengths to recreate a semi-believable impression of ancient Greece, with torchlight and flowing robes and some kind of incense smell, which I still remember to this day. Most memorably of all, they had decided that the play's many deaths should all take place on stage. I found the plot complicated and the central conflict strange and distant from the realities of my own life; but there was a dazzling quality to Antigone's rebelliousness and to the violence and bloodshed that it provoked, no doubt mostly due to the performance of the lead actress, whose furious, tearful eyes burned in the torchlight as if she really were a person prepared to sacrifice her life for her principles, and not just someone playing a part. At one point there was so much fake blood on stage from all the dying that it seemed impossible the performance could continue without someone coming to mop it away. But continue it did, with just about enough time for one layer of blood to dry before another death came along to refresh it. I suppose the message was that blood begets blood; maybe it was a crude way of showing it, but it certainly worked on us.

When the play ended, all the lights in the tent went out. For several seconds, there was total silence, an entire audience left completely speechless – not even the sound of fidgeting, so quiet that it felt as though we had all decided to hold our breath at exactly the same time. When the lights came back on, the whole troupe was lined up across the front of the stage, and suddenly there was an explosion of noise, of people standing up, clapping and shouting 'bravo'. I was sitting between my mother and father, who were still together at the time but – unbeknown to me – already privately discussing their imminent separation. At the end of the performance, my mother must have been the only person there who wasn't clapping, her knuckles gone white from how tightly she was gripping the armrests of her chair, while my father was studiously avoiding looking at either of us. His expression, as he politely applauded the performance, was almost sheepish. I don't think they had expected the production to be so violent – no one had – and they must have felt that they shouldn't have brought me, that I was perhaps too young. I could see other children of around my age scattered among the audience – a few I knew from school, as well as some of the boys from the neighbourhood, my former friends – and their parents looked a little worried too. But the kids seemed thrilled to be there, and I felt the same. I had seen plays before, including previous offerings from this very same troupe, but never anything like this. I remember asking my parents endless questions on the way home: what's fake blood made out of? How do retractable swords work? What happens if they accidentally use a real one and someone ends up dying for real? Do they wash the bloodstains out of the costumes after every performance, or do they use a new set every night? There were going to be three more performances over the next few evenings, and for the duration of that brief and memorable run – and even days after the final performance, long after the troupe had packed up their props, loaded their vans and set off for their next destination – the town seemed unable to talk of anything else.

Naturally, as soon as I found out that they would be back that summer after a three-year absence, I asked my mother to buy us tickets for the opening night, and urged Clara to make her grandmother to do the same. When the troupe arrived, they set up their enormous tent in their usual spot, a sad little park right on the edge of town where every flower looked like it had seen better days, and the grass was so unkempt that nobody ever went there – except, of course, when the theatre rolled in every few years. As my mother and I approached the tent on the first night, I could feel my excitement like a physical sensation in my lungs, expanding in time with the ever-loudening hum of the crowds approaching the theatre tent from various directions – our neighbours and acquaintances, but also people we knew only by sight, and many we had never seen before. It had been announced that this year's production was to be a modern-day stage adaptation of an old folk ballad, but that was all we knew, and so the hot evening air was full of the sound of speculation. I don't know why we didn't just walk or drive over with Clara and her grandmother, given that they lived down the road, but in any event we found them waiting for us by the entrance. My mother swapped her ticket with Clara's so that she and Old Mrs Dickie could sit together and Clara and I could do the same. Clara was grinning, and as she rocked back and forth on the same white shoes I'd seen her wearing the day she'd first arrived in the neighbourhood, I felt a burst of euphoria. We showed our tickets to the man at the entrance – whom I recognized from bit parts he had played in past productions – and stepped inside, making our way towards the front while my mother and Old Mrs Dickie settled into their seats a few rows behind us. Now that we were finally here, it seemed impossible that the fifteen minutes that were left before the play was due to begin should ever pass. We spent some of them discussing the tree that we could see on the right-hand side of the stage. It looked extremely real, but we couldn't figure out how that could be, given that it wasn't in a pot. Had they built some kind of hollow into the stage and filled it up with earth? Or had they literally planted a tree in our wretched little edge-of-town park and built the stage and the tent around it? The other, much more pressing question on our minds was whether the woman who'd played Antigone last time would have a major role in this play too. I had described that production to Clara in exhaustive detail, and desperately hoped that she would get to experience some version of the burning eyes.

The story, when the play finally began, centred on a young man of pure heart but limited means who is hired by a farmer of only slightly less limited means to fix some machinery and help with the harvest. Every day the farmer's daughter – who was indeed played by the Antigone from three years before – brings them some home-made lunch, and very quickly, she and the young man fall in love. The problem, apart from the young man's lack of financial resources, is that she is actually already engaged – to a handsome local man who is only a little older than her, and who is set to inherit his family's somewhat larger and more profitable farming business. So the young woman and the hired hand decide to keep their love affair a secret. As time goes by, the young man develops a closer and closer bond with his employer, who soon becomes a kind of father figure to him. The young woman continues to meet with her fiancé, whom she had been perfectly happy to marry until the day she first laid eyes on her new lover. Her fiancé is kind to her and unfailingly chivalrous, but he is boring and slow-witted, and all she can think of now is the young man she has fallen in love with. As their passion grows, so do the lies they have to tell to hide their secret from the world. And so their love becomes tinged with a bitterness and guilt which they can never bring themselves to speak of. Finally, as the young woman's wedding day approaches, they decide to run away. They will take her father's car and leave in the middle of the night, before they can be found out. When everyone has gone to bed, she takes her father's car keys from the kitchen table and replaces them with a note to explain where she has gone. Outside, her lover is already waiting for her; they get in the car and drive away. Woken by the noise of the car starting in the night, her mother and father clamber out of bed. When they walk past her room, they see that she is not there. Then they find her note. At this point the father looks around the kitchen and sees an empty jug of water on the counter. He walks over to it, picks it up, turns it around in his hands and throws it at the tree, where it smashes into pieces. His wife – the mother – doesn't even flinch.

In the next and final scene, the lovers are driving down a country road at night. They are silent; they have made their bid for freedom, but somehow, there is no joy in this moment. All of a sudden, a dark figure – played by the same actor in the role of the young woman's father – materializes in front of the car. The boy swerves to avoid it, and in doing so crashes the car against the same tree where the jug just shattered, killing them both. The dark apparition turns and stares at the audience for three, maybe four seconds, until the lights go out.

This time, the applause was thunderous and

immediate. Clara and I were clapping with our hands held high above our heads; we kept looking at each other and shaking our heads in disbelief, then turning back towards the stage to cheer the actors – including the lovers, who had climbed out of their wrecked car to link hands with the rest of the cast. They both looked exhausted, but the applause was so enthusiastic that they had to come back on stage three times before it finally died down and people started filing out of the tent.

By the next morning, the town had successfully erased the line between fact and fiction, and convinced itself that the two main actors must actually be in love. Some of our more intrepid neighbours even theorized that they must be in a love triangle of some sort with the man who had played the girl's father – and who was 'certainly not as old as he had been made to look'. How else to explain how true the two lovers' connection had felt to us all, and how powerful, how sinister the look in the father's eyes when he had turned at the end of the play to face us?

My mother raised the subject of the play over breakfast the following morning, trying as subtly as she could to work out whether I'd been traumatized by the shock of that ending. She must have thought I was too young to watch something like that, just as she and my father had feared after they had taken me to that unexpectedly bloody production of *Antigone*. I assured her I was fine and had seen much worse on TV, at which she let out a wry laugh. She didn't laugh very often, at least not when I was around to witness it, and I was surprised to feel within myself a sense of gratification for having elicited some amusement from her.

'Well, I'm glad to hear you've not been scarred for life,' she said. We started discussing the play, the building sense of dread and impending catastrophe that had made it so powerful a spectacle. It reminded her of a show she had gone to see a very long time ago, when she was only a little older than I was now. It hadn't been in our tiny town, of course, but in the big city where she had grown up. She recalled almost nothing of the plot, but she still remembered exactly what the actors had looked like, so clearly that she was sure she would recognize them if they were to walk past her on the street now, all these years later. She also remembered how it had made her feel – how thrilling and disturbing it had been, how it had lingered over her for weeks afterwards like a strange mood. I found it impossible to imagine my mother being anywhere close to my age, so instead I pictured her as I saw her now, tired and distracted but somehow temporarily transformed by this piece of theatre she had witnessed.

'Books make me feel that way sometimes. Only the really good ones,' I told her, and after I said the words, I felt strange, like I was not quite me but a version of me, talking to someone who looked like my mother but wasn't quite her either. For a moment or two, she looked as surprised as I was. Then she smiled, and asked me what I was reading now, and for the fifteen minutes we had before she had to leave for work, and for the first time in what felt like a very long while, we had a conversation.

*

What I remember most vividly about that summer's show was how real it had all seemed – not just the emotions we had watched play out on stage, the love and the jealousy, the fear and the betrayal, but also the physical actions the actors had performed, their kissing, their giddy laughter, even the way they had crashed their car. When the heroine's father appeared in the final scene to stand in the way of the lovers' car, it really did seem like he had come out of nowhere. Clara and I spent an entire afternoon examining my book on optical illusions to see if it might help explain how they'd made it work. We eventually settled on a complicated theory involving a hidden trapdoor, ropes and the ingenious use of lighting. But even more extraordinary than any technical trickery which might explain how the entire audience had seen a man materialize on stage where there had been nothing only a moment before, was the fact that we had all instinctively understood his sudden appearance as being emblematic of something happening beyond the realms of physical reality. This apparition, this figure who had come out of nowhere and whose sudden, hulking presence had ended the lovers' journey in such a violent way, was – of course – a product of the runaway lovers' guilty consciences, their fretful imaginations. And the reason we all understood this so clearly and so immediately was not because it was objectively impossible for the girl's father to have actually caught up with the car, but because every single scene, every interaction we had watched unfold on stage until that moment, had made so clear to us the burdens of expectation, of convention, of obligation under which the two lovers had embarked on their affair. In that context, it made perfect sense that their unconscious minds should release into their own path the ghost of an angry father.

'I think that must be what it feels like to do something

you're not supposed to do. Like carrying a weird ghost around with you that comes out of nowhere one day when you're not expecting it,' I said as we sat on the edge of the creek and cooled our feet in the water. Clara grew thoughtful, breaking into that small frown that I had come to associate with moments when she was talking or thinking about something that was more complicated than it seemed.

'I guess it's also got to do with pretending,' she replied. Her frown began to deepen, and her eyes turned towards the opposite bank, where there was nothing at all to see except for overgrown shrubs and the neighbour's tatty fence.

'It's like, they knew how hard it would be to run away together, how upset everyone would be and how angry her father would be. But also, how will they survive? What happens when the car runs out of petrol? Won't she miss her family? They spend so much time pretending none of these problems exist, or that they just don't matter. It's like they are fooling themselves. But it's like trying to close a suitcase that's too full. You can push the lid down as hard as you want, but if there's too much in there, something will spill out before you can zip it shut.'

'A suitcase?' I said.

'I have no idea where that came from,' she said with

a quick smile. But she soon turned serious again, her gaze shifting back to the clumps of muddy grass across the creek. 'I just think, you can't always be pretending. It's not sustainable. Maybe if they'd just talked about it, how difficult they were finding it, or how guilty they were feeling, the ghost-dad wouldn't have come to haunt them after all.'

'Yes. Though it wouldn't have made such a good ending either.'

'No, that's true,' she conceded. There was a silence, though one filled, as it always was during those summer afternoons, with the sound of water flowing lazily over the creek bed, and intermittent birdsong. I had the feeling, as I often did whenever we ended up talking about anything serious or difficult or in any way complicated, that she was about to say something more, or thinking about saying something more, but weighing up whether she really wanted to or if it would be easier to let the moment slide. It was something in the quality of her silence, a mood that felt more like a pause rather than an ending, and something in the way her body was positioned – with her eyes, her face turned away, but some other part of her body, maybe even just a shoulder or an arm, angled slightly towards me, as if waiting for the words to follow. More often than not, the words never did come, and slowly the errant limb returned to the fold. But not this time.

'I think I do a lot of pretending,' she said, her voice quiet but clear.

'What do you mean?'

'Pretending to be okay, I guess. But in reality I feel worried all the time.'

'Worried about what?'

'I'm not even sure. Maybe that something horrible is going to happen. Also that I won't ever figure out how to feel normal because I'm always worried about something.'

Her eyes flickered towards me before returning to the minuscule whirlpools in the water and the tangle of earth and grass across from us. I could have asked her what else she was worried about. Whether she was worried right now. I could have told her that she did not need to pretend with me; I didn't mind, and would understand. But the truth is that I was scared. It was disconcerting to be reminded so openly that there were aspects of her inner world that I still didn't know about, and that I suspected – on those rare occasions I let myself think about them – of being more unpleasant than I could have imagined. So I didn't say anything. Instead I put my hand on her back and moved it round and round in small circles, like my mother used to do when I was little, like my father had done the time I fell off my bike when I was seven and broke my wrist. She turned towards me and smiled, and when she put her arms around my waist and her head on my shoulder, I felt the same physical burst of joy I had experienced when I had seen her grinning at me outside the theatre tent on the evening of the first performance.

*

Later that night, after I'd had my dinner and watched an old film on TV with my mother, I lay in bed staring at the ceiling and trying to figure out what it was that Clara could have been so worried about. Once again, it was difficult to reconcile what she had told me with my experience of her, but the more I thought about it, the more things I remembered that seemed to fit within the picture she had painted of herself. Times when we had laughed at something together and she had turned around and asked me, hours later, whether the old man standing nearby might have thought we were laughing at him, whether we might have inadvertently hurt his feelings. Or times when we would forget to switch the TV off and the news would come on with tales of some fresh horror, and she would look at me as if to say it could have happened to us, it could still happen to us. It felt like hours before I finally fell asleep, thinking, as I drifted off, about that time we had found a caterpillar in the middle of the road and she had spent fifteen minutes nudging it gently towards the bushes so it wouldn't be trod upon.

8

It was Joe's idea to revive the half-baked plan to play tennis in Old Mrs Dickie's garden that we had made the day the three of us had first met. We discussed how to go about it when we visited his house one afternoon: his little sister was there and begged us to let her join in, but we thought she was too little and we couldn't possibly enjoy ourselves if we allowed her to play with us. 'You can't have more than three people playing tennis in the same place, it's against the rules,' Joe told her. 'Yes, it's forbidden by international tennis regulations,' I added, nodding very seriously, and out of the corner of my eye I saw Clara shaking her head – though she made no effort to intervene, either. I grinned at her, and she rolled her eyes and smiled.

We spent the next morning in her grandmother's garden, trying to figure out how to set up the net in advance of Joe's arrival that afternoon. We found two reasonably sturdy sticks near the edge of the thicket, and some string, but the difficult part was figuring out how best to stretch the string across the two sticks. Too much string and it would sag in the middle; too little and it would pull at the sticks until they collapsed. Eventually we worked out a solution: we planted a third stick halfway between the first two so that we could use two shorter lengths of string instead of a single longer one. It worked perfectly.

Now Joe and I were facing each other across this improvised net. We only had two rackets between the three of us – a pair of battered relics Clara had retrieved from her grandmother's attic together with a single tennis ball – so we couldn't all play at the same time. As we were technically her guests, Clara had suggested that Joe and I go first. Neither of us was a natural, but it soon became clear that I was calamitously bad. Again and again I would swing the racket and miss the ball completely. Sometimes the ball would hit the rim of my racket and spin out behind me, which was somehow worse. The more I concentrated on trying to hit the ball, the more annoyed I got when I missed, and the more annoyed I got, the harder it was to concentrate. Both Joe and Clara kept saying encouraging things, cheering every time I managed to make any contact with the tennis ball, but this felt patronizing, and only served to increase my irritation. I didn't want their kindness; I didn't want Joe to deliberately miss the ball more often than he would've done, or to pretend he couldn't reach the ball one of the rare times I did manage to send it back over the net. I just wanted to be able to do this thing that looked so much simpler when Joe was doing it.

Eventually I grew so frustrated that I gave up. I let my racket fall onto the grass and told Clara she should come and play instead since I was so terrible anyway. I saw Joe rolling his eyes, but much worse than that was the look of concern on Clara's face as I walked off to the side of the court. I ignored her worried eyes. I didn't even want to look at her.

As it turned out, Clara wasn't great at tennis either, but within a couple of minutes she and Joe had managed to establish something of a rhythm, neither trying particularly hard to beat the other and both concentrating mostly on keeping the ball in play. I watched Clara as she gradually worked out the best way to hold the racket, laughing every time she missed a shot and laughing even harder at Joe when he pretended to be gearing up for a big swing only to softly pat the ball so that it soared loosely over the net. They seemed, for a time, to forget I was there. The sun was shining from behind them, and I could see in its glow the fine hair on Clara's forearms. That horrible prickly feeling I knew from nights when I couldn't sleep had come back, like a small wave lapping at my chest from the inside, the pressure lifting a little every time I breathed, only to fall back, heavier and heavier, when I exhaled. Every time the ball hit a racket, hers or Joe's, I felt the thump of it in my chest.

Of course I didn't say anything; there was nothing to say. I just sat there on the edge of the improvised tennis court, mechanically keeping the score. But at some stage I must have gone silent, because Clara suddenly stopped what she was doing and turned to look at me, asking if everything was okay. As I stared back at her, standing there with her right knee scratched from when she had tripped in the thicket earlier, her hair sticking out from beneath the rim of the cap she had worn to protect her head from the sun, the heavy feeling in my chest started creeping up to my eyes.

'Sorry, yes, I think Joe is 4-1 up.'

Clara blinked once, then blinked again, then turned to Joe.

'Shall we play a couple more shots and call it a day? It's so hot.'

I knew what she was doing, but I felt like I might start to cry if I let myself think about it. So I focused on the movement of the ball instead, on the muffled thud it made when it bounced on the grass, on the sweat pooling in the backs of my knees, on the outline of the brown house, stark against the blue, spotless sky.

*

Afterwards, the three of us lay in some shade near the thicket, Joe and I stretched out either side of Clara. Joe was trying to balance a racket on his index finger, without much success. He began to yawn and soon fell asleep. Clara turned her face towards me.

'Are you okay?' she whispered.

'I'm sorry, I don't know what's wrong with me,' I managed to say. I felt like the back of my throat was on fire.

Clara gripped my hand in hers. Her palm was sweaty. There was dirt all over her shoes, and the cut on her knee looked like it had only just stopped bleeding. As she held my hand, the heavy black waves that I had felt spreading through my body seemed to pour into a hollow right on top of my chest. But just as I started to think their weight might become unbearable, they began to retreat. A bird landed on a branch somewhere above our heads and stared at us. I kept my gaze firmly on the bird, but I could feel that Clara was still looking at me. When I finally turned towards her, she broke into a tentative smile. 'If you want we can practise together, just you and me,' she said quickly. I knew then that I didn't need to explain anything, that she had already understood. I told her it was okay; it was too hot to practise anyway.

*

We must have fallen asleep too. I woke up to find Clara curled up against me, with her right arm across my chest, her elbow resting near my navel and her hand balled into a fist on my left shoulder. I lifted my head slightly off the ground and looked down: I couldn't see her face, but I knew from the occasional movement of her eyelashes that she was awake. It seemed to me that if she were to move her arm ever so slightly in either direction, some part of it – her wrist, perhaps, or even the inside of her elbow – would brush against my breasts. I felt hot and sweaty and uncomfortable, and my right arm had gone numb in its enforced immobility, but I could smell the soapy scent of Clara's hair, and I did not want to lose it. I could see Joe in my peripheral vision: he was also awake, holding the tennis racket out flat and rolling the ball around on the strings. I turned my head so I could see him properly, and he stopped what he was doing to look towards me. He lifted his eyebrows and smiled, then asked if we wanted to go and get some ice cream.

NADIA BURST into the galley kitchen looking as excited as Rosa had seen her in a long time.

'Guess what?' she said.

'What?'

'Rowena Tawny and the Sixth Dimensions are playing at the Zodiac Festival and I've got us tickets.'

Rosa had no idea who Rowena Tawny was and had only vaguely heard of the Zodiac Festival, but it was nice to see Nadia in such a cheerful mood. It had been less than a month since they had confronted Goondock's bandits in Renania, and the sombre feeling they had been left with had not gone away. They had not addressed it, but Rosa could sense Nadia being extra careful around her, as if Rosa might burst into tears at any given moment. Even Lynx, whose emotions were always close to the surface, seemed different – quieter than usual, softer and gentler in his movements. Now he was staring at Nadia over his cup of milk, his whiskers quivering uncontrollably.

'Did you … Did you just say we're going to see Rowena Tawny live? The *Rowena Tawny?'*

'I sure did.'

'But how?' said Lynx, still not daring to believe.

'I have my ways,' said Nadia with a smug smile.

Lynx let out a joyful cry, then put down his drink and burst into tears. Nadia came round the table and clapped him on the shoulder.

'Tears of joy, I hope, old friend?' she said, pulling him in for a hug.

'This is the most exciting news I've had in my whole nine lives,' he managed to say in between sobs.

'Who's Rowena Tawny?' asked Rosa.

Nadia gasped, and Lynx was so shocked that he stopped crying.

'Who's Rowena Tawny? Who's Rowena Tawny?' he said, angrily pawing tears off his face. 'Only the most famous balladeer this side of the third galaxy! Only the most beautiful voice in all the solar systems! Only the absolute best!!!'

He burst into tears again. Nadia looked at Rosa with a satisfied smile on her face and a twinkle in her eyes.

'Oh, Rosa, dear Rosa, what rock have you been living under? Who's Rowena Tawny …' she said with a playful scoff. 'Who indeed! You, my beloved friend – you are in for a true celestial treat.'

The tickets Nadia had secured for Rowena Tawny and her band's show at the Zodiac Festival were no ordinary tickets: they came with access to a special area right by the stage, with tables and chairs and even a bar service available. Rosa was sitting next to Lynx and across from Nadia now, drinking the Zodiac Brew the robowaiter had brought her earlier and thinking that life was just perfect. Nadia was wearing a blue velvet cloak she'd announced was 'for special occasions only' and had even left her laserbelt behind. She had also done something to her hair that Rosa hadn't seen before: it shone in the moonlight, sleek and beautiful. Rosa had also tried her best to dress up, and once or twice she thought she caught Nadia looking at her strangely, in a way that made Rosa's heart beat a little faster. But before she could think too much about this, the Sixth Dimensions walked on stage. The noise was deafening, so much so that Rosa thought it couldn't possibly grow any louder – but of course it did, because a minute or so after her band Rowena herself emerged, holding her fiddle in one hand

and its bow in the other, arms stretched wide as if to embrace the entire universe. She was tall and her skin glowed under the purple moon. Her long hair was piled in a swirl on top of her head.

'Hello, Zodiac!' Rowena shouted, and as her eyes roamed over the audience at her feet, Rosa could have sworn that for a moment, the most famous balladeer in the universe had looked right at her and smiled.

Soon Rowena and the Sixth Dimensions were powering merrily through what Lynx informed Rosa were all their greatest hits: 'Someday Somewhere', 'Under the Papaya Tree', 'The Moons of New Yelang', and many more. Rosa had never heard music like it before, slow and meandering one moment, gloriously upbeat the next and with lyrics that seemed somehow to speak to every truth about life and the universe. Sometimes the whole crowd would sing along, and Rosa imagined millions of others across the seven galaxies watching and singing along on simulcast, but even then Rowena Tawny's extraordinary voice would cut through it all, reedy and high-pitched and like no singing voice Rosa had ever heard before. It was mesmerizing.

'Thank you, thank you all for being here,' said Rowena as her band played the last few bars of 'Second Season Blues' – a slow, hopeful number about riding out tough times and waiting for your luck to turn. 'We're going to play you a new

song now – a new song about an old story. A song about love' (this raised a huge cheer from the audience) 'and about longing. It's called "The Ballad of Billy Blue".'

A murmur of excitement rose from the crowd. Rosa could feel it in her bones, the euphoria, the anticipation. There was a surreal moment when, once again, Rowena seemed to be looking straight at her. But it was so fleeting that Rosa was sure she must have imagined it. Then, at a nod from Rowena, the band launched into a brisk but melancholy tune, and Rowena began to sing:

There once was a lad, a handsome lad
Whose name was Billy Blue.
He rode his ship across the skies
And over the waters too.

He travelled away to galaxies far
And planets nobody knew
But he always returned to the loving arms
Of his darling Gemini Sue.

One night, one dark and dreadful night
His ship got lost through and through.
He landed where he didn't expect,
And he didn't know what to do.

A wise old man who saw him come
Said 'Son, you'll be here to stay.
For this storm will rage for twenty years
Before you can get away.'

The song continued for many more verses in which Billy Blue and Gemini Sue, separated by fate and light years, each moved on with their lives, yet never forgot the way they felt about each other. Billy Blue – presumed dead by all who knew him – did not waver in his loyalty to Gemini Sue, while she – who 'sat and wept alone at night / And longed for her lover's kiss' and would 'trade her every silver coin / For one last moment of bliss' – became known for putting potential suitors off by telling them she would consider their advances when she had finished counting all of the stars in all of the seven galaxies. Then, after seventeen Earth Years (three years earlier than the wise old man had predicted), the magnetic storm that had stranded Billy Blue finally cleared and he was able to make his way back to his beloved. When he arrived at what had been and still was their home, at first they did not recognize each other. But then Billy spoke to ask after Sue, and as soon as he did, she knew it was him, for although he had aged, and sorrow and longing had left their mark, his voice when he sang to her was exactly the same.

By the end of the song, Rosa was on her feet, swept away by the same wave of emotion that had taken over the rest of the crowd. Lynx was weeping and banging his paws on the table; it was a miracle his drink hadn't fallen over. Then Rosa looked over at Nadia, who was sipping on her sparkling rice wine with a mysterious smile. They stared at each other for several seconds until the heat from the blush that Rosa could feel spreading over her face and down to her shoulders became intolerable, and she had to look away. She sat back down and took a gulp of her drink to steady herself, and when she looked up again, she saw that Nadia too had averted her gaze. They spent the rest of the evening like that, acutely aware of each other's presence but careful not to let their eyes meet. By the time Rowena's set was over, Rosa felt like her whole body was tingling, alert and conscious in a way she recognized but could not quite name.

They wandered back to the Vela*, talking and laughing and singing the songs they'd just heard, all three of them exhilarated by the show and the collective outpouring of emotion it had sparked. As they sat around the* Vela*'s kitchen table, having a midnight snack and discussing their favourite moments from Rowena's show, it emerged – after much prodding and probing from Lynx – that the reason Nadia had managed to secure those tickets was that a few years ago, she and Rowena had briefly been 'romantically involved'. Unfortunately, their respective occupations meant they had rarely managed to be in the same place at the same time, and eventually they had decided to end things. But they had parted* *on good terms and still kept in touch occasionally. Nadia had recently commed Rowena to congratulate her on the release of her new album, and Rowena had offered her some tickets to the Zodiac show.*

Later, when they finally went to bed, Rosa felt restless and wide awake. She had played it cool in the kitchen while Lynx had teased Nadia over her fling with Rowena. She had pretended to find the whole thing funny, but what she'd actually felt was confused and unsettled, as if something in the configuration of the universe as she knew it had changed irrevocably, yet she was expected to go on as if nothing had happened. She couldn't understand why she was feeling this way; she'd heard stories before – mostly from Lynx – about Nadia's 'conquests' and it had never bothered her. Until today. Nadia hadn't looked like she was enjoying the conversation either, and kept giving Rosa awkward looks. It had been a relief when Lynx, oblivious to the tension in the room, had finally suggested they all retire to their cabins. Rosa spent much of the night tossing and turning in bed, plumping up her pillow in frustration, her mind whirling with the tales Rowena's songs had told, Nadia's uncharacteristic embarrassment, and the unnerving sensation that everything was suddenly different. By the time she fell asleep, it was nearly morning.

9

UP ALONG the creek, a couple of hundred metres upstream from where it bordered Old Mrs Dickie's garden, there was a small, deep pool where the water was slightly warmer and the banks not quite as steep. The pool was surrounded on all sides by trees and so was relatively secluded and almost always in the shade. My father, who had grown up in this town, had told me that when he was little, all the kids would go there on hot days to swim, but then the public swimming pool was built and everyone started sending their children there instead. Now the pool in the creek was always deserted, except during summer evenings, when it became a place where high-schoolers went when school was out to kiss and touch each other. I had seen this myself many summers before – I must have been around ten – when I was still friends with the neighbourhood boys, and we decided to go to the pool after dinner to find out for ourselves whether the stories were true. We'd cut through a wide, empty field that backed on to the creek, and walked along the bank until it curved and disappeared into a small woodland of deciduous trees. The ground here was always muddy and the banks were especially slippery, so we had no choice but to enter the woods and try to follow the course of the creek as best we could. I remember there was a full moon that night, so bright we didn't even need torches to light our way. I also remember how quiet we were – none of the usual chatter, only a single-minded focus on the task at hand. We must have been picking our way through the woods for not more than five minutes when we suddenly saw a glimpse of the pool through a larger gap in the trees. One by one we filed through the gap – five of us in all that night – crouching low so that we would not be seen. Right there, on a small round slab of rock a few metres to our left, a boy and a girl were lying in each other's arms next to a pile of discarded clothes. She had her back to us, and her body blocked most of his from view, except for his hair, which was curly and seemed to stick up in every direction. She was wearing dark underwear – it was hard to know what colour exactly in that light. We couldn't tell whether he was wearing anything at all. They weren't moving much, though we could see in the moonlight that their faces were pressed together, and as they kissed languidly in the night, he kept running his fingertips across her bare back. Their legs were so entangled that it was hard to tell them apart. We were close enough that we could hear the sounds they were making, a quiet sigh, the occasional soft giggle. They were only a few years older than we were but they might as well have landed there from outer space.

I don't know how long we sat there, watching them, but at some point we all found ourselves staring at each other instead. Wordlessly we began to back out of the tiny clearing where we had positioned ourselves, and moments later we were back in the woodland, retracing our steps until we reached the fallow field we had first cut through. I remember looking around at the boys' faces in the moonlight and seeing the same wide-eyed expression I knew I was wearing myself. We walked back through the field, saying very little, and just before we parted ways and prepared to head home, we made a solemn promise that we wouldn't tell anyone about what we had seen that night.

I never did tell anyone, not until I took Clara to the same pool one afternoon that summer. I am not sure what it was that led us there. Old Mrs Dickie's garden was big enough that we could pick a different spot to read in every day – Clara dreamily sighing her way through *Jane Eyre* while I re-read the collection of comic books I had assembled over the years and copied some of the drawings. But we had begun to yearn secretly for a place where we could be alone, and wouldn't have to share each other's company with anyone else. We never spoke about it, but I think we had both come to recognize that there was something singularly intense about our friendship, something that struck other people as odd. We didn't like it when Joe teased us for being joined at the hip. We became defensive when people asked us with good-natured curiosity whether we ever ran out of things to talk about. It was as if we knew they had a point, but we wanted to find out for ourselves what it was.

After that night years ago when I had spied on the boy and the girl kissing in the moonlight, I had only gone back to the secret pool twice, both times during the day. As expected, it had been deserted, and so it was right now. I showed Clara the ledge where the couple had been lying and the gap in the trees where the five of us had huddled to stare, our hearts beating fast with the knowledge that we shouldn't be there, that we were looking at something we weren't supposed to see. We picked our way along the edge of the pool until we reached the ledge. Clara dropped to her knees, peering over the edge of the rock. The water was fairly clear, but deep enough that you could never really see through to the bottom. I sat beside her, dangling my feet over the edge so that the soles of my shoes skimmed the surface of the water. I could feel the coolness of the rock through my shorts and on the backs of my thighs. When I closed my eyes and tilted my face up towards the sky, I felt like the world was holding me gently in its palm. I could hear Clara moving beside me, humming a tune I didn't recognize, then a soft rustling sound followed by two muffled thuds. I opened my eyes to find that she had flung her shoes away and was now sitting as I was, feet slung over the edge of the rock, toes hovering over the water.

I felt in the middle of my chest a spreading warmth, a calm contented joy, like when I was a small child and everything was simple and easy, playing in school with other children as small as me, coming home and practising writing a different letter of the alphabet every day, having an early dinner with Mum and Dad, then off to bed with a goodnight kiss. I'd never really had that feeling again, as if I didn't have to try so hard, and that it was enough to just be, for I was part of the world and the world was part of me. But I felt it again as I sat beside Clara, just as I had felt it since that first afternoon – though fuller and more present now.

'I've never met anyone like you,' I said.

She turned to look at me with something like puzzlement in her expression. I wondered what it was that she thought I meant.

'You're the best friend I've ever had,' I said before she could ask.

She smiled in that way she had, when it was obvious she meant it completely, eyebrows lifting a little so that even her eyes seemed to join in.

'You're the best friend I've ever had too,' she said, tilting her body towards me until she was close enough to rest her head on my shoulder. I closed my eyes again and leaned my head against the top of hers.

Several silent moments passed before she straightened up and turned to look at me.

'So do people ever swim in here, or is it just the local make-out spot?' she asked.

I explained about my father and the local kids who used to come here all the time before the public pool was built. It was safe enough and it was certainly hot enough today, even in the shade. 'But I didn't bring my swimsuit,' I added, feeling suddenly self-conscious.

Clara was quiet for a moment, then shrugged. 'Neither did I.' I watched as she wriggled out of her shorts and pulled her T-shirt and her bra off until she only had her underwear bottoms on. Her shoulders were hunched forward as her fingers gripped the edge of the rock, but I could still see her breasts, her collarbone, her long neck. I watched her slide forward and over the ledge until her toes and then her feet were in the water, her arms straining with the effort of keeping the rest of her body out. Finally, she let go and fell in with a soft splash, letting out a quick, gleeful yelp. She spun around to look at me, then closed her eyes and tilted her head back until it was underwater. I watched a slow, steady trickle of air bubbles forming on the surface of the water right over her nose, until she lifted her head back out and grinned, wiping her eyes dry. 'Aren't you going to come in? It's amazing!'

I looked at her, at her dark eyes catching the warm muffled light that filtered through the ring of trees around the pool, at her hair sticking to her forehead and covering her ears, at her quick, expectant smile. I pulled my feet up over the edge of the rock so I could take my shoes off too. Clara whooped and punched the air, chanting my name as if I were an Olympic swimmer preparing to bring a medal home. I giggled as I pulled my shorts off, then flung my own T-shirt aside and crossed my arms over my chest, craning my neck to peer at the water.

'I promise it's not cold!'

I took a step back, and another, and uncrossed my arms. Then I ran forward and jumped.

*

Later, we were floating on our backs in the water, faces turned up to the sky where thin, wispy clouds lay draped over the blue. Small silent birds kept crossing our circle of sky, tracing strange circuitous routes as they travelled from one tree to the other and back again. I moved my arms in circles to stay afloat, my legs splayed out wide. In the still summer heat, we could hear long-legged insects alighting upon the surface of the water, a sound like soap bubbles popping. There was a branch to my right, or perhaps some kind of overgrown root, that seemed stranded between dry land and water. I made my way towards it, using my arms to swim backwards, until I was close enough to rest my head on the wood. I closed my eyes and spread my arms and legs wide, and felt like a leaf floating untethered across the surface of the earth. Somewhere over and behind my head, a group of birds seemed to be discussing some kind of plan. The water rippled across my chest whenever I made the slightest movement, a pleasant sensation of coolness rising and falling around the base of my neck. When I opened my eyes again and looked down over the bridge of my nose, I saw Clara making her way towards me in unhurried breaststrokes. I thought she would perhaps come to rest with her head beside mine, further up the branch. Instead she kept swimming until she was right in front of me, floating between my outstretched feet. Through the water I could see the tops of her shoulders, the flat stretch of bone beneath her neck. She had pushed her hair back so that it no longer stuck to her forehead, and her eyes were dark and gleaming.

'Can I use you as a pillow?' she asked, using her arms to keep herself afloat.

'Of course.'

I stretched one leg towards her so that she could grab hold of my ankle, then pulled her towards me until she was right in front of my face. She spun onto her back and rested her head just beneath my throat. I could feel her back pressing lightly on my stomach. Her head was heavy, but I didn't want her to move. She wriggled around a little, shifted her head down so that it rested lower on my chest, spread her arms and draped them over and across my thighs. I brought my own arms forward until they encircled her shoulders, linking my hands in the water below her chin. We lay like that, floating in that position, for a long time. We talked about the colour of the trees, about the birds we could recognize and those we couldn't, about the weird insects that kept flying around us, not so much ignoring our presence as treating it as some kind of force field they ought to avoid. Right there, directly in our line of sight, was the ledge we had jumped off, the place where the boy and the girl had been kissing and holding each other that night many years ago. It occurred to me that I was around the same age now as they had been then. I did not know what to do with that thought; it made me nervous all of a sudden, so I tried not to dwell on it.

Clara must have been thinking about them too. 'Have you ever kissed anyone?' she said. I told her I hadn't. There was a boy at school I thought about a lot, though. He was very tall and had broad shoulders and thick curly hair. I had occasionally thought about kissing him, but mostly I thought about touching his arms and about how good he must smell – like laundry detergent. I did often find myself picturing what it would be like to kiss his neck, which looked soft and hard at the same time, and where I was convinced the smell of clean laundry must be at its strongest. This boy was always hanging around with a girl who was in the year above. She was even taller than he was, and had long dark hair, which she wore loose. It looked like hair from a shampoo ad. For a while, the gossip had been that they were secretly dating, but then she had got herself a boyfriend, so we'd concluded that couldn't be true. It seemed they were just friends after all, though the thing I remember most distinctly about her was how unfriendly she was with everyone else in our year, anyone who wasn't him. Sometimes, when I was very bored in class, I liked to imagine that he was my boyfriend. In these daydreams, I wore sunglasses all the time, my hair was long and loose and people were a little afraid of me, though I was infallibly kind to them all and smiled benevolently at everyone I interacted with. His friend from the year above was really nice to me; she wanted me to like her because I was going out with him, and I generously let her sit with us at lunch while secretly feeling superior to her in every way.

Clara listened carefully to this story, which she seemed to find wildly entertaining. Then she told me she hadn't kissed anyone either, though she too had once had a classmate she used to think about a lot. As I stared at the top of her head and glanced occasionally at her toes poking out of the water, she told me about this girl who'd sat two rows in front of her, so that Clara mostly just saw the back of her head. 'She used to wear her hair up all the time, and there were these little wisps of hair on the back of her neck. Sometimes I imagined that I could actually *smell* her neck, that it must smell like soap. And sometimes she would turn her head to talk to the boy who sat next to her and then I would see her face too. I always thought she was so beautiful.'

'What happened?'

'Nothing. She just left. Her family moved so she had to go to a different school. I wasn't upset or anything. I didn't really know her that well. I just always thought there was something very appealing about her, you know?'

I felt like I did know. I knew what she meant. I often felt that way about Clara, when she was laughing about something or reading something out to me, or listening intently to something I was saying; when we lay on the grass in her grandmother's garden and she propped herself up on her elbows and twisted her body around, away from me, to reach out for a blade of grass, and I could see the tiny hairs on her arm and in the dip between her neck and her shoulder; when she put her hands in the creek and wiggled her fingers; when she smiled at something in the book she was reading and her lips pursed, creating tiny hollows at the corners of her mouth. One day we were wandering around town, running errands for her grandmother, when we stopped to rest and hide from the heat under the awning of a grocery store. Clara planted her feet on the ground either side of the pedals of her bike, then crossed her arms over the handlebar and leaned her forehead on her wrists. I couldn't stop yawning, and felt as if I might fall asleep and topple over if I risked closing my eyes too, so instead I ate a couple of strawberries from the punnet we'd bought at Old Mrs Dickie's request. When I asked Clara whether she wanted some, she lifted her head and grinned, eyes still screwed shut, and I remember feeling the force of that smile somewhere in my stomach. Sometimes she would fall asleep in the middle of the afternoon when it was so hot that it felt foolish to be awake, and just before I dozed off myself, I would look at her sleeping face in wonder. I knew these feelings meant something, that they signalled some mysterious condition which I found not at all unpleasant, and for which I had no name.

'You're very appealing too,' I said. It was meant to be a light-hearted comment, or at least I did my best to make it sound that way. When she didn't immediately react, I wondered for a moment whether I'd said something really weird. But then she twisted her neck around until she could just about see me out of the corner of her eye, and I noticed that she was smiling. 'So are you,' she said, and I believed her.

We lay like that for ages, floating in the water and

talking about everything that mattered to us. Eventually the sun had sunk low enough in the sky that we would have been in the shade even without the trees forming a protective ring around us. The air was still warm, but the water had begun to cool now, and I had goosebumps where my skin was not submerged. But it was still quiet, still peaceful here, so we stayed until the sun had really begun to set, only emerging onto the ledge and putting our clothes back on once the sky over our heads had turned a light shade of purple.

10

A COUPLE of days after our first visit, we returned to the shaded pool, and this time we took Joe with us. We had played tennis with him again after that first time – I still couldn't be relied upon to hit the ball more often than I missed it, though I didn't mind so much anymore – but the weather only seemed to be getting hotter, so that day we decided to go swimming instead. Clara and I gave each other piggyback rides across the pool and chased after Joe. I remember her legs wrapped around my waist, her knees digging into my ribs as I pushed my arms through the water, and then the feeling, when we swapped around and it was my turn to be ferried around, of her back pressing up against me. I kept seeing flashes of a recurring dream I'd been having, with the outline of a person – a figure I knew and felt to be me – lying in a dark room, cool water rising slowly around them, a sensation like fresh bedsheets on bare skin. I always woke up just as the water was about to submerge the figure completely, and even though the nights were hotter than they had ever been in my life, I would lie there shivering until I fell asleep again.

Eventually Clara pleaded exhaustion and clambered back out onto the ledge. I stayed in the water for a while longer before swimming towards the ledge myself and leaving Joe to float contentedly on his back at the opposite end of the pool. I gripped the edge of the rock and pulled myself up until I could hook my leg across it. As I pushed myself clear of the water, I noticed that Clara was staring at me, her eyes focused not on my face but somewhere around my shoulders. I looked down at my own arms, slick with pond-water and quivering with the effort of bearing my weight. When I turned my face back up, she was looking straight into my eyes. I had seen that expression on her face before – at first only when she must have thought I wasn't looking, but increasingly also in moments when I was quite obviously aware of what she was doing. But it was only then, as I threw my leg over the edge of the rock and managed, with one final push, to scramble out of the pool, that I realized she was looking at me exactly the same way I had begun to look at her.

A few days later, Clara and I kissed. We had gone deep into the thicket to escape the sun, and what little light filtered through did so unpredictably, so that you could be one moment in semi-darkness and find yourself squinting against the light the next. We had spent the morning soaking our feet in the creek and talking very little. This was a new kind of silence between us, different from the lazy, quiet hours we had spent reading or sleeping side by side next to the creek or in the garden. This silence was heavy and full, bursting with something unknown. The longer it went on, the more obvious it became – to us both, I'm sure – what it was really about. All it needed now was for something to happen that would break it.

We found a place under a tall, leafy tree with a thick enough canopy to shelter us from the worst of the heat. Forest dust floated in the air around us, the smell like the inside of a flowerpot. Moisture stuck to our hair and clung to our clothes. Clara was wearing a faded old T-shirt I had grown to love, with the picture of a famous aquarium in a foreign country and a stylized puffer fish emerging from the blue. The kind of thing my mother, or anyone's mother, would have relegated to the status of pyjama top, never to be worn where anyone else could see. Naturally, Clara wore it all the time. We spread our blanket at the foot of the tree. Clara sat with her back leaning against the trunk and beckoned at me to sit beside her. We had brought our books with us to read, but left them in the bag along with the bottle of water and the peaches Old Mrs Dickie had given us to pack. The silence continued, thick and expectant. I sat next to Clara. The tree trunk wasn't quite wide enough for us to both sit side by side, so I angled my body towards hers. She was resting her head against the tree, eyes closed, legs folded up and pulled against her chest. She looked relaxed, but I could see that her hands were gripping the blanket. All around us the woodland crackled, thick with the scent of sap and moist earth and heat. I could smell Clara's shampoo through it and hear her steady breathing. I placed my hand over the back of hers and felt her grip on the blanket tighten. She opened her eyes and turned to look at me. She was so close now that I could only look at one part of her face at a time. I knew exactly what was about to happen. I closed my eyes and pressed my lips against hers.

I had no idea what to do next, but then something took over, some elemental instinct. When the tips of our tongues touched, my arms and then my whole body began to shake. I could feel it between my legs, like I did at night sometimes, or when I was back home from school and alone on dark winter afternoons.

We pulled apart. Our faces were so close that I couldn't focus on her properly. Our noses kept brushing against each other. I was out of breath. I felt sick. I wanted to do it again. All around us, the life of the thicket continued. In between bursts of birdsong, we could hear the creek bubbling in the background, and an occasional rustling in the undergrowth suggested the presence of other beings sheltering from the heat. Clara put her hand on my shoulder as if to steady herself, then moved even closer, so that the side of her body was pressed against my chest. She nestled her face in my neck and wrapped her arms around my back until any remaining space between us disappeared.

'That was amazing,' she mumbled into my skin.

I closed my eyes and smiled.

*

We spent the rest of the afternoon talking and kissing under the tree. Clara kept stroking my hair and I kept running my hands up and down her arms. It was early evening – though not dark yet – when we heard Old Mrs Dickie's voice calling out to us from the garden. Our hands were clasped together as we picked our way through and out of the thicket. We had held hands before, but this was different: now our fingers were interlaced and the feeling of her fingers pressing into the spaces between mine was so vivid that it felt like another way of kissing. We only let go when we were about to emerge from the treeline. Old Mrs Dickie waved us over and suggested I stay for dinner. She had done this a few times now and I had always demurred, but this time I knew I must stay, otherwise the past few hours might end up feeling like something out of a parallel universe that wasn't quite our own. I remember everything about that dinner, the stained salmon-pink tablecloth, the blue-rimmed plates, the pasta salad ('goodness me, too much salt! Sorry, girls'), Old Mrs Dickie asking me studiously unprobing questions about my family and whether I liked school, and Clara and I sitting side by side, our legs pressed together as we told her grandma about the spot where the creek gathered into a shaded pond, how lovely and quiet it was, a haven compared to the public pool. Old Mrs Dickie had not lived here when she was young, so I told her what my father had told me about how it used to be the prime swimming spot and how, after the opening of the public pool, it had become a place where high-school kids went at night for their secret rendezvous.

'And you two like it there, do you?' she said, surveying

us with an indulgent look in her eyes. I remember blushing at the question and Clara giggling next to me before mercifully taking over. 'Oh yes, Grandma, very much so. We'll show you one day when you're not too busy gardening.'

'I'm always busy gardening, my dear. You two enjoy your pool. I think I remember things always used to be more fun when there were no grown-ups around.'

There it was again, that indulgent smile hovering benevolently on the edge of laughter. I felt such a surge of affection for her then, this woman whom I had never even spoken to until that summer, who looked so old, and who seemed to have figured out somehow that the best way to build a relationship with the granddaughter she hardly knew was to appear when she was needed and to otherwise let her be, let her roam around the house and the garden and the whole town with the strange, quiet girl she had befriended.

Cycling the short distance home that evening, I felt like I was gliding. I could feel my heartbeat not just in my chest, but in my arms, in my legs, behind my eyes. I was looking at the road but I kept seeing flashes of the day, our silence in the thicket, Clara's lips against mine, hotter than the air around us. It was like when something bad happens and your mind keeps going back to it, forcing you to relive the discomfort over and over until it's lodged in you forever and you've figured out how to live with it – except this was the opposite kind of feeling, an all-consuming elation, the most amazing thing that had ever happened to me. I almost felt as if I ought to ration the thought, so I kept trying, as I cycled home, to think of other things too. It worked for a few seconds at a time, and every time I allowed my thoughts to drift back to where they really wanted to dwell, the pleasure seemed heightened, like when you are sitting outside on a hot sunny day and a trail of clouds moves in across the sky to bring you shade and respite from the heat.

When I came home I found my mother asleep on the couch in front of the TV. I switched the TV off, but she didn't stir. We kept a thin blue blanket on the back of one of the armchairs. My father had used it to cover his feet in winter. Now that he was gone, nobody ever used it anymore. I picked it up and draped it over my mother, then turned off the lights and went upstairs to my bedroom, where I fell into a swift, undreaming sleep.

11

Thinking back on that summer now, I can see how every day we had spent together had led us inexorably towards that point. Even then it had felt like the least surprising, most obvious thing that could have happened. When you spend that much time with somebody, and when that time begins to feel so intensely charged with some kind of secret, nameless energy, the sense of a physical separation between your body and theirs seems almost to erode, until it begins to feel strange not to be touching them in some way or not to feel them touching you. That was why, when we found ourselves dozing on a picnic blanket in Old Mrs Dickie's garden, we would curl up against each other despite the heat; or when it was actually too hot to be outdoors, and we lay instead on her grandmother's sofa, watching TV, I would rest my head on Clara's lap and she would thread her fingers through my hair. She wouldn't even move her hand; it would just stay there, fingertips pressing gently against my scalp.

There had been times over the course of the previous weeks when, lying beside Clara on a shady bank or in her grandmother's garden, I had experienced a sense of cellular dislocation, some invisible yet substantial part of my being removing itself from my body and attaching itself to Clara's until I was overcome with a sense of expectation – as if I had leapt off a diving board from an infinite height and was now hanging in the air, forever waiting to break the surface of the water. After we kissed for the first time, that feeling only intensified. Until then, it had existed as something nameless and inchoate inside me, so bound up with everything else that I had always longed for and found in her that I couldn't really separate it from all the rest. Now, any distance from Clara suddenly seemed too great. Merely being close to her was not enough. When she laughed, I felt the vibrations in my own throat; when she wriggled her toes in the grass, I felt my own feet tingle. I wanted to absorb her, press her so tightly against me that we would meld into one.

The next day was the hottest we'd had all summer. People were warned to stay indoors unless they had to go out, and if they had to go out, to avoid the hours between 10 a.m. and 3 p.m. and if they couldn't avoid those hours, to at least wear a hat and loose clothing, and drink double the amount of water they normally would.

Clara and I went up to her bedroom. It was cool in there, the closed blinds keeping the sun out and steeping the room in a kind of half-light. It was so hot outside that the birds had stopped chirping, and we could distinctly hear the sound of the creek. The room was painted green and sparsely decorated – a nondescript guest room, with a small wardrobe against the far wall and a chest of drawers which doubled as a dressing table. But there were traces of Clara all over the place. There was the backpack she'd brought with her from home and that I had seen her clutching to her chest the day she'd arrived; a pile of books she had found in her grandmother's library, stacked in a neat tower at the foot of the double bed; a small heap of discarded clothes piled onto an armchair next to the window. And there was Mr Lego-Man, standing proud on the bedside table. Clara dived across the bed to retrieve him, holding him aloft as she twisted around on the mattress and pushed herself up to sit with her back against the headboard.

'I'm so glad I finally get to meet Mr Lego-Man,' I said,

sitting cross-legged in the space beside her. 'He's even more handsome than I thought he would be.'

Clara laughed as she put him back on the bedside table, then shuffled forward and spun around until she too was sitting cross-legged in front of me. She was still smiling, but there was something different in her expression now, a look of anticipation. Silence again, the creek in the background and a clanging from the kitchen, where Old Mrs Dickie was busy sorting the herbs she had picked from her garden early that morning. Clara took a deep breath and opened her mouth as if to say something, then closed it again and looked away towards the foot of the bed, still wearing that same cryptic half-smile. I put my hand on her knee and she turned her gaze back onto mine. Her skin felt soft and warm and a little sweaty under my palm. She looked serious now, a little tentative, but there was that glow in her eyes which I had seen the first day we'd met and nearly every day since. I had the same feeling I'd experienced when cycling home the day before: as if I had not one heart in my chest but five or six of them scattered across my body, all thumping at exactly the same time so that it felt as though someone had placed some kind of drum inside me. She closed her eyes and leaned forward.

*

This is what I remember of the days that followed: kissing for hours on the ledge by the secret pool, breathing each other's breath, jumping into the water to cool down, resurfacing to kiss again; reading side by side from the same frayed paperback copy of *Pride and Prejudice*, Clara always reaching the end of the page a few seconds before I did and spending those seconds rubbing her forehead and her cheek against my shoulder like a cat; watching television in Old Mrs Dickie's living room when it was too hot to be outside, kissing Clara's fingertips and slipping my hand up the back of her T-shirt. We would always spring apart whenever the noise from the kitchen stopped and we thought Old Mrs Dickie might be about to walk in. But I don't remember having any sense that we were doing something wrong, something to be ashamed of; rather, it seemed impossible that anybody could understand the intensity of what was happening to us, and so it was much simpler to be left undiscovered. We felt as people often do when they are in love: that nobody had ever felt as we did, so profoundly connected, so in need of each other. I remember we talked about it once, speculated on whether this was 'normal', concluded that it wasn't. Clearly we were special. It seems a sweet, innocent thing to think, and of course it was. We were not the first two people to fall in love, nor would we be the last. But we had gone from feeling lonely and out of place and wondering what it was that we needed to do differently, to finding that all of that had suddenly fallen away. I do not have the heart, now, to smile at my younger self, nor to dismiss what she knew to be true.

I remember our first sleepover: my mother's surprise when I asked her if I could stay at Old Mrs Dickie's, her palpable relief that her daughter was doing something as normal as staying the night at her best friend's house. Old Mrs Dickie made some kind of lentil salad for dinner, then went to bed to finish the murder mystery she was reading. We had promised her we would do the dishes, and now Clara was standing at the sink, methodically cleaning plates and cutlery while I stood behind her, leaning my body against hers with my eyes closed and my head turned to one side so that my ear was pressed against her back. I listened as she scrubbed the last plate, then rinsed everything and placed it carefully on the drying rack. I felt her shoulder blades shift as she reached for the tea towel, and once she had dried her hands she turned around and wrapped her arms around me, sliding her cool, slightly damp fingertips under the hem of my T-shirt. We went upstairs to her room and changed into our pyjamas with our backs to each other. I suppose we were still shy and didn't quite know how we were supposed to behave. Then we lay side by side and turned the bedside lamp off. We started talking, our voices low so as not to disturb Old Mrs Dickie, but also because it seemed unnatural to talk at a normal volume while lying there, staring at the ceiling in the dark. We were so close that our arms were pressed against each other. I lifted my hand and moved it so that it was resting on her thigh, and she began to run her fingertips up and down my forearm.

'I had a horrible dream last night,' she said, turning her face towards me. 'There was an earthquake, we had to get out, I thought you were right behind me, but then I turned around and you were gone and I had no idea where you were. I thought you were dead. I was so happy when I woke up and realized it wasn't real.'

I felt that tingling warmth again, spreading across my chest and up to the tips of my ears. I turned around and kissed her.

*

I woke up in the middle of the night. There was a rustling outside the window, some nocturnal creature scurrying across the garden, but other than that only silence and the creek in the background, as constant as the passing of the hours. I was disoriented at first, but not for long. Clara was right beside me, fast asleep. The pillows, the air, the entire room smelled of her – of soap and shampoo and the scent of her skin. It seemed to have concentrated in the night, pooling in the space between us. I reached out to touch her shoulder, then moved closer and pressed my nose, my mouth against her neck. Then I fell asleep again.

When I woke up in the morning, I knew exactly where I was. I looked at Clara, curled up beside me with the bedsheets tangled around her legs and her hair sticking to her forehead, and I felt like a bird must feel when it is gliding across the sky, held aloft by some invisible current in the air, the forces of the universe conspiring to ease its journey.

Rosa heard the laser beam before she saw it.

'Take cover!' she yelled instinctively. There was a split second in which she saw Nadia and Lynx hesitate, but then they managed to dive behind a large boulder – just in time for a second, better-aimed laser beam to graze the top of Lynx's left ear.

'Ouch!' he yelped, rubbing his paw furiously against his singed fur. A group of locals and aliens who had been waiting in line outside the tavern across the road scattered into the evening.

'What the hell was that?' said Nadia.

Rosa ducked behind a corner a few feet from where Nadia and Lynx were crouching. She thrust her hand into her kit bag and found one of the RecoRoaches she had bought – at great expense – from the local tech exchange. She crouched to the ground, tapped her personal code into the Roach's back, and released it. Thirty seconds later, the Roach was back with all the information they needed.

'It's Goondock and his lot again,' she muttered just as another volley of laser beams targeted the rock Nadia and Lynx were huddled behind.

'They must be out for revenge. How many in total?'

'Seven – four diagonally to your right, and three straight ahead. They have old-model laser guns and they are hiding behind some parked hovercars.'

'Shit. What do we do?' said Nadia. Another barrage of laser fire hit the rock, chipping a worryingly large piece off the edge. Lynx did his best to return fire, but with limited room for manoeuvre and almost no vision, none of his shots landed.

'Have you got any light bombs on you?' Rosa asked Nadia – as quietly as she could, so that their attackers wouldn't hear.

'Yes – two.'

'Great. We need to create a diversion and then we run into that alleyway over there. I'm pretty sure it leads to the main square. Hopefully those people who were queuing for that tavern will have called the enforcers by now, so all we need to do is buy ourselves some time.'

Nadia and Lynx nodded. It was a good plan. Nadia pulled

out a light bomb from the pouch hanging from the back of her laserbelt and lobbed it over the rock so that it landed right in front of the hovercar behind which most of Goondock's gang was hiding. Three seconds later, there was an eruption of dazzling brightness. Rosa, Nadia, and Lynx took this opportunity to run as fast as they could into the alleyway Rosa had pointed out, their retreat threatened by a haphazard cascade of laser beams. There was a moment when Rosa felt a searing pain somewhere around the back of her left shoulder, but it was gone in an instant, overpowered by the rush of adrenaline that came from running full pelt down a narrow street and the thrill of having outsmarted Goondock's bandits yet again. Within seconds they had reached the city's biggest square, which was always crowded at all hours of the day and night, and minutes after that they were back on their ship, in the safety of the heavily guarded spacedock. Goondock couldn't reach them here. They were safe!

It was only after the entrance ramp of the Vela *hissed shut behind them and they stopped to catch their breaths and take stock of the situation that Rosa remembered the pain in her shoulder. It was back with a vengeance, piercing and impossible to ignore. She couldn't see anything on her chest, but she could feel that the back of her shirt was wet. Something on the floor near the edge of her foot caught her eye; she turned around to take a proper look and saw that it was blood, shining crimson under the lights of the ship's loading deck.*

'Rosa? You're bleeding!' she heard Lynx say.

'Am I?' she replied.

'Rosa!' he cried, and that was the last thing she heard before she fainted into his arms.

When Rosa came to, she found herself lying face down on her bed aboard the Vela. *Nadia was sitting on a stool beside her; Rosa could only really see her knees, but from the sting and the repeated pressure on her left shoulder, she guessed Nadia must be biohealing her wound. Apart from the slight burning sensation, the feeling was strangely soothing, and Rosa nearly fell asleep again – until Nadia reached a spot she hadn't previously touched, and the sudden piercing pain sent a jolt through Rosa's body.*

Nadia leapt to her feet so quickly that she knocked the stool over. Now she was hovering over Rosa from three feet away, as if she were scared of coming any closer.

'You're awake,' she said, her eyes darting from Rosa's face to her shoulder and back. She was still holding the BioLancet she had been using on Rosa's wound. Rosa had never seen her look so scared and helpless. It tore at her heart.

'Yes. I was having a really nice dream, actually, until you started jabbing at my shoulder with that thing,' she said, forcing a chuckle.

But Nadia didn't laugh.

'You could have died,' she said instead.

'It's just a scratch. I'm fine!'

'But you could have died. A few inches lower and it would have gone straight through your heart.'

Nadia's eyes were brimming with tears. In all the time she had spent alongside Nadia, Rosa had only seen her cry twice: once when Nadia had twisted her ankle so badly that Lynx had had to carry her to the nearest RoboClinic, and once when a little boy they had rescued from a fire that had spread through his village on Antigua-VI had asked them if he could go back inside his burned-down house to look for his baby brother. Rosa felt a desperate need to reassure her.

'It's okay. Honestly, it's fine – it doesn't even hurt anymore, look,' she said, but as she tried to push herself up and roll onto her side, a fresh burst of pain seared through her injured shoulder, and she fell face down back onto the bed. Nadia was still standing a few feet away. Her expression had hardened, and her whole body was shaking with repressed emotion.

'What do you think you're doing? You can't do that yet. You need to lie down,' she snapped.

'But I've got a crick in my neck.'

'I don't care about your neck. You need to rest.'

The anger in Nadia's voice, harsh and unexpected, hit Rosa like a physical blow. She felt it in her chest, and suddenly she was the one fighting back tears.

'Nadia ...' she pleaded.

But Nadia's fury was like the tip of a knife, sharp and unyielding. She squeezed her eyes shut for a moment, as if she couldn't even bear to look at Rosa. Then she opened them again, and they were filled with such awful anguish that Rosa understood it was really herself Nadia was angry at.

'You nearly died and it's my fault. I put you in danger. I should never have taken you from New Saturn.'

Now it was Rosa's turn to snap.

'Taken *me? You didn't take me anywhere. You asked if I wanted to join your crew and I agreed. You didn't make me. You didn't force me. And you're not putting me in any danger that I'm not willing to put myself in.'*

'But if we'd never met, then at least you'd be safe,' said Nadia, her voice cracking.

'If we'd never met, I'd be on my own, trying to figure out how to get through another day. How to keep warm. Where to find food. You don't know what it was like for me, how difficult it was. Not really. But now ... I didn't even know it was possible to live like this. You changed my life, Nadia, and I wouldn't give that up for anything.'

The tears spilled out now and Nadia was crying too, unable to hold her own tears back any longer.

'I don't want to lose you, Rosa. You mean so much to me. I don't think I could bear it.'

Rosa stretched her arm out, ignoring the pain in her

shoulder, to reach for Nadia, and the next moment Nadia was kneeling on the floor by the bed, her head level with Rosa's, her hand clutching Rosa's so tight that it hurt. It occurred to Rosa that it was the first time since that night at the Zodiac Festival that Nadia had touched her. Before that night Nadia would often put her arm around Rosa's shoulders, or link her arm through Rosa's as they strolled through the capital of some planet they had never visited before. But over the past few weeks they had danced around each other like opposing magnetic poles, Rosa unconsciously avoiding contact too. It felt good, now, to have bridged that distance. It felt right.

Rosa squeezed Nadia's hand back, feeling in her heart and in every bone and muscle in her body that there was no force in the universe that could ever tear her and Nadia apart.

'Look at me, Nadia. I'm here. I'm right here. I'm not going anywhere.'

12

Two weeks later, Clara was gone.

There had been signs, of course. Some I hadn't noticed at the time; some I had deliberately ignored, like that absent, inscrutable look she would get when we talked about her family, how she seemed to become smaller somehow, to shrink into her shoulders. Her voice would go quieter, her face would turn blank – no smile, no frown, only an unreadable nothingness, as if her eyes had suddenly lost focus. It was horrible to have to watch this happen, a painful, helpless feeling of wanting to reach out and take her face between the palms of my hands but not knowing whether it was the right thing to do. I desperately wanted to make things better, to remind her that she was not alone and that I was here now. But I would never ask her what was wrong. It's so hard, when you're young, to see beyond your own feelings for long enough to know what to say and how. It was easier to assume it must have something to do with her parents going away all summer and leaving her behind. So I would say something funny or splash some water in her face until she laughed and her eyes came alive once more. Only later, long after that season of my life had passed, would I come to recognize and regret the failure of courage, the selfish, paralysing terror which had prevented me from allowing those silences to settle into truth.

But other signs had been as inescapably obvious then as they are now. There had been that afternoon a few weeks into the summer, well before we had kissed for the first time under the tree in the thicket, when Old Mrs Dickie had walked up to us in the garden and asked Clara to come inside; her father had called on the telephone and was waiting on the line to speak to her. I glanced at Clara and realized her face had gone completely blank in that horrible way I had seen before. She got to her feet as slowly as if her limbs had been burdened with thousands of invisible weights and she was having to cast them off one by one. She didn't say a word to me, just walked across the garden and towards the house with her grandmother's arm around her shoulders. She didn't look back once.

Old Mrs Dickie came outside again a few minutes later. 'You should probably go home, dear,' she told me. 'This might take a while.'

I gathered my stuff and left, feeling like a child. Something bad was happening, something secret and upsetting, but nobody was telling me what was wrong. Did they think I wouldn't notice or did they just not care either way? I heard nothing as I walked through the house and out the front door. Either the phone call was over, or it was taking place in some hidden corner of the house, well out of earshot.

When I returned the following morning, Clara opened the door and gave me a long, silent hug. She smiled at me, but I could see straight away that it wasn't real, a show of false cheer that made me feel sick and helpless with foreboding. I had seen her smile like that before. I found it hard to look at her when she did it, because I knew it meant that there was something deep and dark beneath the surface of things that she couldn't explain or that she thought I wouldn't understand. She said nothing about what had happened the previous day, and I didn't ask.

Then there had been that brief, unsettling conversation we'd had one afternoon many days later. We were sitting by the creek, feet dangling in the water. The earth and grass felt cool against the backs of my legs, and a large, leafy tree beside us provided some relief from the heat. Clara's hand was resting on my lap. I had been spelling words out in her palm with the tip of my index finger, and kissing her every time she guessed correctly.

'I wish you could just move here permanently,' I said. 'Then we could go to school together. We'd have so much fun.'

She gripped my hand in hers so that our fingers became intertwined. I turned to look at her but she was staring down at the water. With my free hand, I began to trace new words on her forearm. *I'll miss you. I love you*. She turned to look at me, and I could see the tenderness in her expression.

'I love you too,' she said.

I watched her eyes move across my face, as if she were checking against the picture she had of it in her mind. She was smiling, yet although it was a true smile this time, it was also terribly sad, suffused with some kind of unsayable truth. I thought I understood. Sometimes, despite my best efforts to ignore it, the thought that Clara had to leave and go home eventually would surface in my mind like a wave of desperate panic, and all I could do was wait for it to pass.

'Don't be sad,' I told her, though I could have just as

easily been talking to myself. 'We still have nearly half the summer left. And you can come and visit in the holidays. Or I could come to you.'

I thought we'd talk about how we would arrange this, what we would do if she came back here, what she would show me first if I went to visit her. Instead she unclasped her hand from mine and pulled her arm away, crossing it over her chest and clutching her opposite shoulder. She turned away, lowering her head and closing her eyes. She lifted her feet out of the water and pulled her knees up, curling her body into a ball. I did not know what was happening, though I think some part of me must have understood, even then, that this was not the same sadness that I was feeling. I placed my hand on her back, between her shoulder blades, but she didn't move. I remember that very clearly, because I touched Clara all the time now, every day, and she always curled into my hand like water pooling into a bowl. But in that moment it was like I wasn't even there and she had gone somewhere else, beyond my reach, leaving behind only this strange, immobile likeness.

'Clara,' I whispered. 'What's the matter? What's wrong?'

'Nothing,' she said, mumbling into her knees.

That was the first and only time I'd ever asked her anything like that directly, and the only time she'd had to lie to me. I've often wondered since what would have happened if I'd kept asking – whether she would have kept lying to me over and over again, or if she would have finally told me the truth.

I moved my hand slowly up her back until it was resting on her neck, and this time I felt her body respond, like a long-held breath let out. She began to straighten up, dipped her feet back into the water, uncrossed her arms.

'It's nothing. I'm just sad because I'll miss you.'

She leaned her head against my shoulder and closed her eyes. I remember how unnaturally quiet she was for the rest of that day, and every now and then I would catch her with this strained, desperate look on her face that made me feel, again and again, as though I was missing something obvious and enormous that was happening right in front of my eyes. I had seen that expression before, quivering like the surface of the water in a glass filled too close to the brim, eyes staring into nothing, seeing nothing except perhaps whatever was playing inside her mind, invisible and unknowable to the rest of the world. I had seen it on my father's face before he'd left, I had been seeing it on my mother's face all my life when she thought nobody was paying attention. On Clara it looked completely incongruous. How could a person who laughed like she did, as readily as she did, hold tucked away within them such a vast capacity for sorrow? I couldn't fathom it then, though now I know that I had things the wrong way round. Despair lived inside of her: it had its own room, bigger than the others, and sometimes it ventured outside and ambushed her. The wonder was that she could keep it at bay at all, that she could laugh as she did and as often as she did despite its lurking presence.

But these were things I came to understand only much later. I did not yet know how life can sometimes resemble a war of attrition between joy and misery, where the armies of the latter are better equipped and more committed to their cause, and whatever truce we might be lucky enough to have negotiated does not guarantee protection against its incursions. All I knew back then was that something seemed to happen to Clara in certain moments, something beyond my grasp, that separated her from the realm of ordinary pleasures and preoccupations, even though she might deny that it was so. The strange thing was that I could tell there was something important that she wasn't telling me, but instead of trying to prod and poke at the truth, I decided to avoid it – as I had done all those other times that summer when I had watched her fold inward like a paper boat sinking into the water. Here was this thing I didn't know and couldn't name, out of sight but so heavy that it warped the air around it. To look at it, to drag it out into the open, would change everything. I couldn't face it. So I pretended – to her and to myself – that it wasn't there.

Later that afternoon we'd picked our way down the bank towards our secret pool. We'd taken our clothes off and carefully lowered ourselves into the water to float on our backs, a silence lingering between us. Then, once our swimsuits had dried, we'd got dressed and returned to her grandmother's house. I hadn't stayed for dinner, but when I'd gone back the next day we'd pretended again as if nothing had happened.

*

Our last day was absolutely ordinary, but I remember everything about it. We spent the morning swimming in the shaded pool, kissing on the ledge, seeing who could hold her breath underwater the longest. We had forgotten to pack the sandwiches Clara's grandmother had made for us, so we returned to the house for lunch. Old Mrs Dickie had left to run some errands in town and told us she wouldn't be back until the late afternoon. We sat on the sofa and watched soap operas until our favourite cooking show with the greasy-haired chef came on. When it was over, we went up to Clara's bedroom and read for a little while, until we realized it was too hot even for that. We decided to go out on our bikes and buy some ice cream from the little shop near the bus station – lemon ices for us both. On the way back we ran into Joe's mother, who invited us to come round for the peach sorbet she had made the day before. We spent the rest of the afternoon watching Sheba run in circles around the garden while we played our own made-up version of poker with Joe and his little sister. Joe's sister got upset every time she lost. She was still too young to have learned the secret rule the rest of us had long since figured out: that you are supposed to pretend you don't care whether you win or lose. I remember Joe and I teasing her for it and Clara giving us reproachful looks as she told her that it was all right, it was only a game, and her luck was bound to turn. We made sure to keep playing until it did.

'I was just like her when I was little,' Clara told me on the way home. 'I couldn't stand losing.'

We'd stayed until it was almost dark and the sky had turned that muted blue it acquires at twilight sometimes when the weather is clear and the air is warm, making the outline of things, of street corners and lamp posts and electricity cables, starker somehow, even in the failing light, so that you end up feeling like you might have wandered onto a film set, none of it quite real.

'I still hate losing. I don't think I'll ever grow out of it,' I said. We started talking about something vaguely related – something to do with school, playground games we had won and lost. It felt no different from any other conversation we'd had that summer, though she had a surprisingly serious look on her face, eyes staring straight ahead as if she were pondering some vital and terrifying question. She came all the way to our front door. I asked her if she wanted to come inside, maybe stay for dinner, I was sure my mother wouldn't mind. She told me she should probably head home, her grandma would be expecting her. I think I said, 'See you tomorrow.' I don't remember whether she responded, but I do remember that she smiled and stepped forward and hugged me for what felt like a very long time. The back of her T-shirt was damp with sweat, and she smelled of grass. I felt like I was holding the most precious thing in the world; I felt a soft, easy joy spreading through every part of my body. Then she let go and picked up her bike and began to cycle away. I smiled when she looked over her shoulder and waved at me, and watched her all the way until she went round the back of her grandmother's house and out of sight.

I stepped inside. My mother had been too tired to make dinner, so she'd ordered pizza instead. It arrived a few minutes after I did. We ate on the sofa in front of the TV, mostly in silence, but there was an old comedy on and we kept laughing in the same places.

'Did you have a nice day today?' she asked during a commercial break. I told her how we had gone swimming in the morning and spent the afternoon at Joe's house. I didn't say anything about the home-made peach sorbet; I didn't want her to feel bad.

'Can I invite Clara for a sleepover?' I asked.

'Of course, peanut. It'll be nice to finally meet your friend.'

*

When I arrived at Old Mrs Dickie's house the next day, Clara had already left. She had been picked up earlier that morning by a taxi her father had arranged for her. That is what Old Mrs Dickie told me when she answered my knock on the door. I still remember how surprised she looked when I asked her where Clara was. Had Clara not told me she was leaving?

She had not. I thought she must have forgotten.

'When will she be back?'

The expression on Old Mrs Dickie's face shifted into something resembling pity. She was quiet for a moment. I began to feel a creeping fear in my stomach and in my chest.

'She's not coming back. Her mother's been discharged now, and her father thought it best for Clara to come home too, so she can prepare for the new school year.'

A dark wall of dread began to rise within me; I could feel it pouring out of my face and my arms like sweat and spreading into the hot morning air. I became oddly conscious of my breathing and my heart – how they both seemed to be speeding up even though I was standing still. My stomach felt like it was collapsing on itself, tendrils of heat creeping down my legs and up into my throat.

'I'm so sorry, dear. I thought she'd told you.'

'No. She didn't say anything. Is she really not coming back?'

She looked terribly sad, and I remember thinking, in a strange, detached sort of way, that she must be feeling very sorry for me. It didn't once cross my mind that some of that sadness must be for herself.

'Why don't you come inside and sit for a moment? I have some lemonade left from yesterday. I'm sure Clara will write or call as soon as she's settled in. You've been such a good friend to her. She must be missing you already.'

She was smiling now, a sad smile that warmed her eyes. That awful, prickling heat inside my body intensified. I was going to cry. I did not want to cry. I could not go inside, into Old Mrs Dickie's soft familiar living room, and cry like a child as I sat on the sofa where I had spent so many hours that summer watching TV with my head on Clara's lap. So I told her I had to go home. I picked up my bike and cycled away.

THE END came out of nowhere. No warnings, no sirens – only the sound of a massive explosion followed by countless smaller ones, the ground shaking, chaos and panicked screams as people tried to run for cover but found that the very buildings they'd thought to shelter in seemed to be crumbling at the edges under a barrage of sonic cannons. Droneships criss-crossed the sky, firing rockets at one another and spiralling to the ground when they were hit, so that within minutes it seemed as if the sky itself were coming apart. In the distance, a colossal flying vessel decked in carnival colours was crashing as if in slow motion, fire spreading across its surface as it fell inexorably towards the ground. A cruise zeppelin caught in the crossfire.

Nubia and New Carthage had been at war for three years now, and their conflict had wrought death across their solar system. But this city, this city with its sunny canals and lush mangrove forests, this city where, until moments ago, Rosa and Lynx and Nadia had been sitting in a little café drinking sparkling lemonade and planning their next adventure, had always been neutral territory. Not anymore: from one moment to the next, it had become a battlefield.

Nadia sprang into action.

'We need to get to the spacedock. Now,' she said. They started running along the canal, crouching low over the ground, ducking and weaving their way through piles of debris. All around them people were running for their lives. There was a woman with a small child in her arms; Rosa turned to ask Lynx if he could help her, then turned around again just as a stray rocket exploded right in front of the woman. Rosa saw her own horror reflected in Lynx and Nadia's faces, but there was nothing they could do. So they kept going. The noise was relentless, rockets and droneships crashing into trees, into canals, into restaurants and cafés and people's homes. Then a blinding flash of light, followed by the sound of another huge explosion – the ground itself was shaking again and they had no choice but to stop running. They looked up and there it was, one of the motherships – Nubian, judging from its shape – looming large in the sky, its shields and cloaking systems clearly now damaged, but its launch chutes

still spawning droneships and its energy beams still firing at an enemy the civilians on the ground couldn't even see.

Another rocket exploded somewhere behind them, and had it not been for Lynx's reflexes, they would have all been thrown to the ground. They started running again, Lynx bounding ahead on all fours to scan for obstacles before doubling back to help them through. It was impossible to fully grasp what was happening. It did not seem real, and soon Rosa began to lose her sense of the present. She was still moving, still keeping up with Nadia and Lynx, but in her mind all she could see was the cruise zeppelin engulfed in flames, the woman with the child in her arms, the flash of light from the damaged mothership.

They followed the canal until the small civilian spacedock finally came into view. Almost there now – almost there. If they could just make it back to the Vela*, if they could just take off, they would be okay. They would fly close to the ground to avoid the droneships, and once they'd managed to escape the fighting, they would be able to leave the planet altogether. There were only a couple of hundred yards to go now. They could see little fires burning across the airfield, a huge cargo vessel with a rocket-shaped hole in its side, and people, dozens and dozens of people, all scrambling to find a ship that would fly them to safety.*

'How many can we take?' Nadia asked Lynx as they hurried onward.

'Depends – I'd say six or seven, so long as she's not been damaged.'

Finally, they saw her – the Vela, *standing unscathed exactly where they had left her, in one of the bays reserved for private spacecraft. Rosa saw Lynx and Nadia's faces light up with joy and relief. She watched them sprint ahead, then duck for cover as a droneship pierced the sky overhead with a telltale whistle and crashed into the woodland that bordered the spacedock. She saw the moment Nadia realized that Rosa hadn't kept up with them, saw the panic in her face when she turned around to look for her. Nadia called out her name, but Rosa couldn't hear her. It was happening again, the feeling that she wasn't really there. Nadia was the woman with the child now, and in the sky there was a flash of white light and a cruise zeppelin burning as it fell to the ground.*

Then she saw them: four rockets heading towards the airfield. Perhaps they had been fired there on purpose, or perhaps their intended target had been the droneship that had just crashed nearby. Rosa watched as the missiles approached, saw the people on the airfield frantically looking for cover, heard Nadia screaming at her to run. There was a terrible sound. Rosa felt a wave of heat pass over her and her body lift up as if raised by some invisible mechanical hand. When the hand finally returned her to the ground, she lay there, blinking, until the sky above her turned white.

13

I SPENT the rest of that day in my room, sitting on the floor at the foot of my bed and watching as the line of light slanted through the shutters and moved along the wall. I looked at the objects around me, staring in turn, for seconds at a time, at the bottle of sunscreen that had rolled underneath the armchair, at the wardrobe I'd left slightly ajar, at a pair of socks on the chest of drawers. Joe knocked on the front door and called my name, but I ignored him. My mind kept returning to Old Mrs Dickie's sad eyes, circling her words as if to parse them for some secret meaning I had previously failed to grasp, and all the while my body throbbed with a pain that was not quite pain, but more an unrelenting pressure, as if a second body shaped exactly like my own had wrapped itself around me and begun, ever so gently, to squeeze.

The light had dipped all the way to the bottom of the chest of drawers when I heard my mother's sandals clicking on the porch, her key turning in the lock, her handbag landing heavily on the shelf by the door. She didn't seem to realize I was home. I must have left my bike round the side of the house. I heard her wash her hands in the kitchen sink, then open the fridge and sigh. If I focused hard enough on those sounds, I could almost see her moving around the kitchen, chopping vegetables, placing a pan on the hob, the same actions day after day. A few minutes after she walked in, the phone rang. I could hear every word my mother said into the phone and I figured out almost immediately that she must be speaking to Old Mrs Dickie. My heart was hammering in my ears, and I began to feel sick.

'Oh dear. No, I hadn't heard. Goodness, I had no idea. Poor thing, how awful. It must have been a difficult time for you all. Yes. Well, of course, that certainly makes sense. I am glad to hear she is better. Of course. Yes. I understand. Yes, of course. I will speak to her. Thank you for letting me know. And please call if there is anything we can do.'

She hung up, and for several seconds there was only silence and the thumping of my own heart. Then I heard her coming upstairs, her footsteps getting louder as she climbed closer. I knew what was coming. I didn't want to hear it. But it was there now, hanging in the air like a tree that's being cut down, about to topple over. My mother knocked on the door.

*

This is what she told me: around two months ago, about a week before the end of the school year, Clara had come home to find her mother lying unconscious on the bathroom floor, an empty box of pills beside her. It was a Wednesday; Clara was supposed to be on a school trip to the theatre that evening, but it had been cancelled at the last minute. Clara's father had been away on a business trip for the last few days; he was due to land in the late afternoon.

Clara had called the emergency services. They had taken her mother to hospital, and this prompt intervention had probably saved her mother's life. Clara's father had come home from the airport to find the retired couple who lived across the street now sitting in his living room, looking after his daughter until he arrived. Clara and her father went to the hospital right away, where they found out that Clara's mother was already awake and expected to make a full recovery. But by then she had heard what had happened – that it had been her daughter who had found her – and when Clara and her father walked into the hospital room, the sight of Clara proved so distressing to her mother that her father had to take her straight back out. It was therefore decided that Clara should be sent away for a short while, at least until her mother was discharged and had recovered more fully. Clara's father had two brothers; one lived with their elderly mother, who had dementia and needed round-the-clock care, and the other was married to a woman who resented any contact he had with his family. Clara's mother had a sibling too, but he lived abroad; it did not seem practical to send Clara so far away. The most logical solution had been to call upon Old Mrs Dickie, even though she and her daughter were practically estranged, and she had not seen her granddaughter in four years.

Three weeks ago, just over a month after the 'incident', Clara's mother had been discharged from hospital. Of course she had not meant for Clara to find her. In fact she hadn't meant any of it – certainly nothing quite so 'drastic'. It had been something of an accident. Old Mrs Dickie had not spoken to her directly – only to her husband, who also reported that his wife was getting stronger every day, and would soon be well enough for Clara to come home. And so, last night, Clara had packed her bags, the books she'd brought from home, and all the daisy chains she had made for us that summer, and in the morning she was gone.

14

THERE WERE exactly two weeks left until the start of school, but time had now become one long loop, every day beginning and ending in the same way, impossible to distinguish from what had come before and what would happen next. The joy of those long days with Clara faded almost immediately. Though the images remained intact and more vivid than ever, they made for a desolate picture now, their persistence a constant reminder of what was suddenly absent. I kept having dreams where Clara appeared wearing clothes I had never seen before, and did nothing, just stood there in silence, staring at something beyond me, even when I shouted out her name. Sometimes her hair looked different; sometimes her face did, though I always knew it was her. I would wake up in the morning and lie there with my eyes open for what felt, in the violent, unyielding heat, like hours. I was grateful that she had never come to my house, that we had never watched TV in my living room or kissed and napped through the midday heat in my bedroom; I was not sure I would have been able to survive the daily reminders otherwise. Sometimes it felt like I had forgotten how to breathe. Sitting on the porch rocking chair, I would stare sightlessly at the book I was meant to be reading and try to catch my breath. It didn't work, my lungs never seemed to fill, the harder I tried the worse it was, on and on like that until something happened, a car drove down the street or a squirrel crossed the road, to distract me from the shallowness of my lungs and allow my body to remember what it had always known to do without direction.

There is a passage in *Jane Eyre*, one of a handful I remember reading over Clara's shoulder that summer, where Jane has just discovered that Mr Rochester, whom she had believed she was about to marry, is in fact already married, and that his wife has been living all this time hidden away in the attic of their home. *A Christmas frost had come at midsummer; a white December storm had whirled over June …* When Jane locked herself in her room, overcome by a state of desperate disbelief, her misery, I realized, was twofold. It wasn't just that her dreams of happiness and love and security had been dashed; it was also that she had lost Mr Rochester as she knew him. *Mr. Rochester was not to me what he had been; for he was not what I had thought him.* How could he have not told her? How could it be that she should discover through somebody else, and almost by accident, this heavy, lurking secret at the centre of his life? If she hadn't known this, then could she say she had ever known him at all? As I sat alone in my room or on the porch day after day, some invisible force pressing into my chest and back and bearing down on me from all sides, one of the few feelings potent enough to filter through the fog of my shock was something I can only describe as a sense of abject mortification. I had told Clara things I had never told anyone else, I had thought through things with her I had hardly thought of before. I had shown her every part of me and thought she had done the same. I had trusted her completely, but she had shown me only a version of herself and left out something enormous. Now she was gone and I was alone again, with nothing left but the humiliation of it all.

I became a detective, obsessively replaying moments in my mind in search of clues. I spent hours thinking about every conversation we'd had that summer, every afternoon by the creek, every laugh and every kiss, trying to understand how I could have missed this, what I could have done differently, when she'd said one thing but meant another. When she said I was her best friend, was she only saying that because she didn't know anybody else here? When she hugged me for the last time, had she held on for longer than usual or had I imagined that too? The worst part, the most sickening thing, was the suspicion that I had been too much somehow – said the wrong things at the wrong times, made the wrong jokes; that I had been wrong to think her affection for me matched mine for her; that I had been wrong to assume that she must be waking up in the morning feeling as excited to see me as I was to see her. Had she been bored all along, only pretending that she was enjoying herself? How much had been true and how much of it had she put on? I think some part of me knew that it wasn't as simple as that, but it felt easier, sometimes, to believe she had faked it all.

The other feeling I remember from those days is anger. Surely she had known, surely she could tell how much I had depended on her, on her friendship and her love, and still she had betrayed me. I dreamed one night that I was at school and Clara was there too. There was no classroom; we were all outside on the pavement and on the street, cars driving past us. The teacher had told us to pair up with a classmate. I looked for Clara but I couldn't find her. I crossed the road and she was there, sitting under a tree, wearing her aquarium T-shirt. Before I could say a word, she told me she'd already found someone, then stood up and crossed back over to the other side of the road. She looked so cold, like Clara's face but with someone else, some stranger, behind it. I woke up with a jolt and lay there, curled up on my side, trembling with silent fury. I started having imaginary conversations with her, endless arguments where I laid out all the ways in which she had let me down, accused her of being a liar, and berated her in excruciating and perfectly constructed detail for being a terrible person. I kept returning to these conversations in my head, refining my arguments, coming up with increasingly elaborate scenes of verbal vindication, and producing ever more scathing responses to her attempts at defending herself or explaining why she hadn't told me. I often pictured Clara returning to find me and Joe swimming in the creek close to the shaded pool. She wanted to join us, to play with us. In this particular scene, we were children – it made no sense, and yet it felt exactly right. She would come and stand on the edge of the creek, she would call out to us, but we would ignore her, we'd pretend she wasn't there, only she would know that we were pretending because I'd make sure to look at her and then to look away with all the indifference I could muster. So she would call out again, only my name this time, and I would tell her that it was fine, she could join us if she really wanted to, but when she did we would simply continue to ignore her, both of us, Joe and I, in full agreement that she had behaved abominably and deserved nothing but disdain. On and on in this way, fantasies in which I would pour all my mortification onto Clara until she burst into tears, chastened and remorseful. But that was always where these consolatory visions seemed to falter, for whereas I might have set out picturing some final act in which I would magnanimously offer Clara my forgiveness and feel good and righteous about the generosity of my spirit, I would find instead that by the time I made it to the end, the scripting of these imaginary confrontations left me confused and exhausted. Then I would lie in bed or on the floor and stare at the wall until something happened – a sound from outside, a bird landing on the windowsill – to rouse me from my stillness and focus my mind once more on composing all that I would have liked to say to her.

Three days after she left, Clara telephoned our house.

It was late evening, the sun had set and the air was marginally cooler than it had been all day. I was in the living room watching TV with my mother, paying undue attention to what the figures on the screen were doing. Every scene and every line of dialogue seemed vitally important, for I was afraid of what might occur, how I might start to feel if I allowed my mind to wander, and I did not want this to happen in front of my mother. We had not spoken about Clara again, not since that first night when she had come up to my room to tell me what had happened and why Clara was gone, and even then I hadn't said a word – just listened to her story then told her I wanted to be left alone.

People often rang our house, and unless it was my father calling to talk to me, it was usually my mother they wanted to speak to. So when the phone rang that night, she got up to answer it. I remember the warmth that crept into her voice as she spoke to the person calling, and when she said 'How is your mother doing?' I knew immediately who it was. I kept my eyes fixed on the television but all of a sudden I seemed to have lost the ability to follow what was happening, like reading the same paragraph in a book three times over and still not taking any of it in. I heard my mother put the receiver down on the shelf and walk back towards the living room.

'It's Clara on the phone. She's asking to speak to you.'

'I don't want to speak to her. Tell her I'm not here.'

'Darling ... it's ten thirty. She knows you're here. Don't you want to know how she's doing?'

I looked up at my mother's face, her sad, perplexed expression.

'I don't care. I don't want to talk to her.'

She looked like she was about to say something else, but then changed her mind. I watched her turn around and walk back to the telephone, heard her tell Clara that I wasn't able to come to the phone. The feeling of wrathful satisfaction that had come over me when I had refused to go to the phone had already dissipated, and now I just felt numb, as if I had used up my full reservoir of feeling. My mother came back in and sat on the opposite end of the couch. She seemed disappointed. I imagined this must be the face she made whenever one of the kids she looked after did something they weren't supposed to do.

'I don't know why you're looking at me like that. She lied to me and then she left, except *I* didn't do anything to deserve it.'

I wanted her to shout at me, to tell me off, but she did neither of those things. She just looked at me and frowned.

'I'm going upstairs. Don't stay up too late,' she said.

I sat and stared at the screen until the movie was over and another one had begun. Then I climbed up the stairs in a daze, lay on my bed, and searched my mind for some kind of emotion, for anger, or contempt, or maybe even resignation. But there was nothing there.

15

Clara called twice more that week. Each time, my mother picked up, and each time I made her tell Clara that I couldn't come to the phone. Then the letter arrived. I had been sitting on the porch all morning, holding a book without really reading it. I kept thinking of the feeling of reading shoulder to shoulder with Clara, of the smell of her skin and her hair as she waited for me to catch up, how she would smile at me and her eyes would crinkle up with contentment. When the postman handed me the letter – a rare piece of mail addressed to me – I knew straight away that it was from her. Perhaps I had been expecting it. I stared at it, sitting unopened on my lap, and tried to imagine its contents. I am so sorry I never said anything. They told me I mustn't talk about it. But I was wrong not to tell you. I miss you. I don't know what I'll do without you. I wish you were here. I know I made a terrible mistake. I betrayed the best friend I've ever had. I know you must hate me now, but I hope some day you'll be able to forgive me. Last night I dreamed that we were on the ledge by the pool and you were kissing me and when I woke up I was crying because I missed you so much.

I stood up and went inside, the letter heavy in my hand. I stepped into the kitchen, pressed the thick envelope against my face, into my eyes, and breathed in. Then I walked over to the counter and placed the envelope in the kitchen sink. I opened the cutlery drawer where my mother kept a box of matches. I lit one and lowered it carefully into the sink. The envelope caught fire, and I watched it burn until it was completely consumed.

*

The next day Joe came by when I was sitting on the porch, so that I couldn't pretend I hadn't seen him come or heard him knock.

'Hi,' he said.

'Hi.'

'Why have you been avoiding me?' he asked, lowering his bike to the ground.

'I don't know what you're talking about,' I replied, shielding my eyes from the sun.

'Yes, you do. But never mind. I miss Clara. She was great,' he said.

'Yes. She was.'

He was looking at me as if he expected me to say something more, but I was determined not to fill the silence. My sense of self-control was already precarious, and it felt especially dangerous to be talking to Joe, who had spent so many days with us that summer, and whose words could have easily shattered the protective barrier of indifference I had been trying so hard to erect.

'Is she doing okay?' he said eventually.

'I don't know. I haven't spoken to her since she left. I'm sure she's fine.'

His eyes widened for a moment, then narrowed as he frowned.

'Did you two have some kind of fight?'

By then I'd had so many fights with her in my head that I had begun to wish we'd had one in real life. Anything would have been better than this absence. But I said none of this to Joe.

'No. We didn't have a fight. She just left without telling me.'

'So you had no idea any of it was going on?'

I shook my head and looked down at the book on my lap. I couldn't even remember what it was that I'd been trying to read.

'Shit,' I heard him say. 'That sucks. Are you okay?' he asked.

I lifted my face to look at him, and a voice came out of me, forming words of its own accord.

'Whatever. It's fine. She was only here for the summer anyway. She would have had to go back eventually.'

'Still, that's—'

'I told you it's fine. I'm going to go back inside now; it's too hot out here. I'll see you around.'

I slipped out of the rocking chair and walked to the door. Joe watched me without saying a word. After I stepped inside and shut the door behind me, I heard him pick up his bike and slowly pedal away. I climbed up the stairs thinking of nothing at all, an empty space where feelings ought to be, and the sensation that I was not really me, just someone who happened to look and walk like me. I had the fleeting thought that Clara would have known what to say to make me feel better, but of course I could never speak to her again. I lay across the bed and fell asleep, and dreamed that Clara had come back on Joe's bike and we were all eating ice cream and walking along the bed of the creek. Sometimes the water reached above our ankles. Other times it barely covered our toes. All around us there were birds chirping in the trees, and every now and then we saw tiny fish darting through the silver water. When I woke up to the sound of my mother's key turning in the lock, there was a moment when the world of the dream was still real – not so much the scene itself, but what it represented, all of us together again, Clara returned, perhaps never gone at all. Then the present fought its way to the surface again, and when I remembered the truth, my whole body curled in on itself, and I felt so tired that I was sure I would never move again.

*

A few days later my mother came in after work one evening and told me she had run into Clara's grandmother in town. Clara's mother was reportedly doing well. Clara's father had requested a transfer to a different department that would require significantly less travel. Clara was coping as well as could be expected, and had asked whether I had received her letter. I told my mother that I had, but that I'd been too busy to reply. She didn't say anything else at first, and was quiet for so long that I had no choice but to turn and look at her.

'I know you're upset that she left without warning. But you need to understand that sometimes people's lives are more complicated than you think, and there are things they might not be comfortable telling you about. That doesn't have to mean they don't love you or value you or whatever else it is that you're thinking. I can see that you're hurt, but if you care about your friend you should pick up the phone and call her. I'm sure Old Mrs Dickie would give you her number if you went round to ask.'

It was the most she or anyone else had said to me in days. Some dark, twisted feeling spiralled within me, a black, miserable rage that made me want to pick up the glass of water I'd put on the coffee table and fling it at her.

'Shut up. You have no idea what you're talking about,' I said. She didn't respond, just stared at me for a moment, then turned around and went into the kitchen to heat up leftovers for dinner. We never spoke of Clara again.

*

That night, three days before the start of school, the heat broke. There was a thunderstorm, more rain in two hours than we had seen in months, and afterwards, just like that, the days were less suffocatingly hot and the nights cool enough to require light blankets. There had been talk of little else all summer, but within hours of the change in weather, nobody was even mentioning the heat anymore. It was all forgotten.

16

THE MONTHS after Clara left were the worst I've ever experienced. I have never known misery like it, and although I have since experienced times of objectively greater difficulty, it has always been the benchmark against which I have measured any periods of prolonged sorrow in my life. It was visceral and all-consuming, a black hole at the centre of my private universe that I didn't have the words to describe, that I didn't even want to describe because I didn't think anybody could grasp its magnitude. It was all I could think of and it made everything else seem inconsequential, so that I felt I could do nothing else but keep feeding it. What was the alternative – to ignore it? That was unfathomable.

To think about it was to know that it was there, and even though it was impossible, at that time, to separate the joy of those summer weeks from the bleak anguish that had followed, it was still better to acknowledge that they had happened.

In time, the darkness began to clear. Sometimes that thing we secretly fear, that horror we can scarcely bear to think of, does come true, and we lose somebody we love more than we have loved anyone else before. Some losses are more difficult than others, and each is terrible in its own way. Yet even when we think we can't possibly live to make it through to what awaits on the other side, we usually do. Time continues to pass, our lungs fill with air, we shiver when it is cold and sweat when it is hot. The scenes I pictured in my mind when I couldn't seem to do anything else, or when I couldn't sleep at night, changed from desperate confrontations with Clara – the only person I wanted to talk to, but also the person I held responsible for my misery – to elaborate, often tragic re-imaginings of stories set in the worlds of my favourite books, just as Clara had told me she used to do with Nadia and her crew. Sometimes I appeared in these scenes; sometimes Clara did; but more and more as time went by, it was the characters from the books themselves who featured most prominently. I would dwell on some moment of particular jeopardy or of dramatic separation for much longer than the books did, and thus, as I arranged close-ups in my mind of the hero's bitter tears or the heroine's anguished expression, my own sadness began slowly to be subsumed into a broader arc, as old as literature itself, of sorrow and loss.

I began to make some friends at school – two girls who had been there all along but whom I'd never spoken to properly before. I started talking to them during a lunch break, entirely by accident. There was something going on, some kind of commotion on the basketball court. It was the kind of thing Clara would have found funny. They found it funny too, and from that day on we always spent the lunch hour together and started meeting up after school too. I am sure that this would not have happened had I not met Clara. I would not have given those girls a chance; I would not have given myself a chance. But now I knew that there was nothing wrong with me, that I was not alone in the world. There were other people a little or a lot like me, and just because I hadn't met them yet, it didn't mean I never would.

One year passed, then another. I still dreamed of Clara, especially on hot nights when the feeling of a clammy, caved-in pillow must have jolted something in the palace of my memory. These were always rancorous, difficult dreams from which I would wake up feeling as if I had done something wrong – though as time went by their frequency diminished, as did their power over me. Clara did not return for any of the school holidays, and the year after, Old Mrs Dickie sold her house and moved away to be closer to her daughter – with whom, after a long period of estrangement, she had finally reconciled – and her granddaughter. In those three years I occasionally received news of Clara – mostly through Joe, who would casually pass on anything his mother had heard from Old Mrs Dickie. Clara's mother remained well. Clara had taken up competitive swimming. She was excelling at school, and had been accepted into a prestigious foreign university. Joe would deliver these updates, then pretend he hadn't said anything at all, giving me however much time he thought I needed to compose myself. But after Old Mrs Dickie moved away the news stopped coming, and eventually the memory of the summer I had spent in her garden and the time I had shared with her granddaughter crystallized into something that belonged in an increasingly distant past.

Joe grew into a kind and generous man with a boring job that allowed him to devote most of his time to his friends and family. By then both of us had long since moved away, but whenever we met up and talked about our home town and the summers we had spent there, we would talk about Clara too and speculate on what she might be up to. But there was always something left unsaid. The first and only time we had a frank conversation about her was at his eldest daughter's wedding, more than forty years after that first summer. He told me that day that he had always suspected that Clara and I had been in love, and had always felt guilty for not saying anything about it after she'd left. He had not known how, and he'd been scared of making things worse. I told him that it didn't matter, it had been a long time ago, but that it was true: I had loved her, and she had loved me, even though for a time, in my anger, I had persuaded myself otherwise. Then she was gone, and I was left feeling as if I hadn't known her at all, and as if none of the things I had experienced had been quite real.

But I had understood eventually what my mother had been trying to tell me all those years ago, the last time she ever mentioned Clara, though I had not been prepared, in that moment, to recognize the truth in her words. No matter how deeply you love someone, no matter how much your sense of self becomes intertwined with theirs, you are not them and they are not you. We think we know other people, but we only know what they themselves know and what they will allow us to see. There is always a separation, an empty space that cannot be breached, but it is the work of friendship and love to try nonetheless, to look as far as we can see and be neither discouraged nor resentful when we reach the limits of our vision. The people we love may not always behave in exactly the way we would want or expect them to, but that doesn't necessarily mean they do not love us as much as we thought they did. Sometimes it just means that there is something in their life that we simply cannot know.

'I wonder what she's doing now,' said Joe.

I had tried looking her up on the internet once, many years before, when it suddenly seemed possible to find anyone in the world. But Clara had a common surname, which yielded what looked like an endless series of results, and I couldn't recognize her in any of the photographs. Perhaps it had been too long; perhaps I wasn't looking hard enough. I never forgot the letter I had set alight in the kitchen sink – the letter whose unknown contents I had long since imagined and memorized, and to which I had often returned, in the first few months after Clara's departure, whenever I felt alone or aggrieved and it was soothing to think of how I had been wronged. That letter would have contained Clara's address or at least her parents' address, though I am not sure I would have done anything with that information anyway. Why hadn't I tried harder to find Clara? Certainly there was a part of me that had hoped, at least initially, that she would be the one to reach out, to try again. But I had also been embarrassed – ashamed of my anger and how I had allowed it to eclipse every other feeling, so that it had never even occurred to me to listen to my mother, to set my own misery aside and try to imagine what Clara had gone through, what she was still going through. By then I had long since forgiven Clara; it took me a lot longer to forgive myself, though I got there eventually too.

Over the course of the years, the memories of my weeks with Clara, clouded temporarily with bitterness and disappointment, recaptured their original brightness – if tempered somewhat by the passage of time. The summer I spent with her became a story I told close friends and sometimes lovers too, a story of how I discovered friendship and love for the first time, then lost them both again. But there was only the faintest trace of sorrow left in its telling, and no regret. I have never regretted meeting Clara. I never did, not even in that terrible time after she left, when I found myself questioning if I had fundamentally misunderstood what I had meant to her. I may have imagined, in those weeks and months, countless scenarios in which I was the one who walked away from her, had the last word, crushed her spirit in the way I felt she had crushed mine. But I never wished I'd never met her. That summer I learned what it means to love somebody so much that it feels like you might actually be the same person, with a different face and a different voice, but with the same beating heart.

17

'THERE'S A man here who's asked to see you. He says he needs to talk to you. He says it's about someone called Clara. Shall I let him through?'

It has been a long time since I last heard that name, but I have been thinking about her more and more as the years go by and distant memories become clearer somehow. Perhaps that is why I am not as surprised as I should be that someone has turned up at my workplace wanting to speak about her.

Moments later, the visitor is standing in my office, a tall man with greying hair who looks like he might be in his thirties. He is holding a backpack in one hand, and when he stretches out the other to shake my hand

and introduce himself, there is something familiar about his eyes, a gleam that cuts through the shyness, warm and mischievous. He says that he is Clara's son. He has been looking for me for the last two years, ever since his mother passed away. He tells me it has not been easy to find me, and I can understand why: I changed my surname when I got married, and even after I was widowed I never changed it back. In the end it was a stroke of luck that led him to me. He had set up a search alert for my maiden name – which, like Clara's, is fairly common – and after numerous dead ends, it had yielded a result for a paper I had published many years ago, before I was married, but that had been quoted more recently in a book on children's literature. The same book quoted another paper I had published later, under my married name, on the series of books about the space explorer Nadia. Once he had realized that the two versions of my name belonged to the same person, Clara's son had followed this lead to find a brief biography, which mentioned my home town – the same town where his mother had spent an eventful summer many years before. That was when he knew for sure that he had found the person he had been looking for.

'My mother tried to make us read those books when we were little,' he tells me now. 'They always felt a bit dated, but it was clear how much she loved them. Her eyes would light up.'

'Like yours,' I say.

He smiles. 'I know. People always say that I look nothing like her, but the eyes are the same eyes.'

They are the same eyes. We have been standing all this time, but I feel light-headed all of a sudden, so that I end up having to sit on one of the chairs across from my desk. He seems unsure what to do, asks me if I need anything, a glass of water perhaps. I wave him off and gesture at the chair opposite me. He sits down.

'What happened to your mother? How did she die?'

'She had been ill for many years. We all knew it was coming. But we got a lot more time with her than we could have hoped for, so I suppose we were lucky.'

'Did you look after her?'

'No. My dad did. He nursed her close to the end when it was really bad. I think she was as comfortable and happy as she could have been. We're looking after him now, though. They'd been married for so long he's not used to being alone.'

'They must have been good friends.'

He gives me a strange look, as if he were trying to work something out.

'Yes. They were best friends. She always used to say to us, there's no point having love without friendship. She used to say that's where it all starts, that it's hard to sustain love without it. Though when I look at my father now and see how lonely he seems even when we're there, I wonder if maybe that's not so sensible after all.'

He is smiling as he says this, as if to suggest he's joking, really, but I can tell he is unsure. I wonder whether he is with someone, whether he's happy. He is silent now, leaning forward in his chair with his backpack between his feet, waiting for something. He turns his head towards my desk, examining the pile of marking he has interrupted, the unopened chocolate bar I was planning to have later in the afternoon, the back of a photo frame. I let him complete his survey. When he turns his gaze back on me, I see a glimpse of Clara in his eyes again, and I have the feeling, as in a bad dream, that I have arrived too late and something really important has passed me by, though I can neither name it nor remember what it is. The not remembering, the not knowing, somehow makes the feeling worse.

'Why did you come here? Why have you been looking for me?'

It is a blunt question, but I try to make it sound

gentle, so that he understands that I am asking even though I already suspect the answer, so that he knows that he can talk about his mother as much as he would like to, even though I knew her for so little time, even though, in the scheme of things, I hardly knew her at all. But when I look at him again, I see that he does not look sad, only curious, and maybe even a little hopeful. The answer he gives me is not the one I was expecting.

'I wanted to find you because towards the end of her life, in the last year or so, my mother started talking about you all the time. She said you were the first friend she ever had and the first person she really loved. I remember one day in particular. Me and my sister were sitting with her and Dad, watching a movie together, and something must have reminded her of you. She started talking about you again, how much she had loved you, and we were saying how sweet that was, how special to experience a friendship like that, and then she turns to us and stares and says no, no, you don't understand. I *loved* her. We were in love. I remember looking over at my father who was sitting with her feet on his lap and smiling at her with so much love in his eyes. I figured he must have heard the story before. Fifty years on and her eyes were still lighting up at the memory. She was always tired by then, often in pain, but when she talked about you and that summer you had together, she looked younger somehow. We couldn't understand how she had never told us about you before. My sister … we realized my sister is named after you. She was actually angry about it for a while when she found out – how could you name me after this person you never even bothered to tell me about? That sort of thing, you know. But then my father told us the parts she hadn't yet explained – how she'd left without warning, how she had tried getting in touch but you never wrote back, and she didn't press you because she thought she would have probably done the same in your shoes. I remember thinking, asking him, aren't you jealous? She talks about this person like they met yesterday, like she still loves her. He just burst out laughing. He said, of course she still loves her. You don't just forget that kind of thing. But it was a lifetime ago. I love your mother, and that girl she met that summer made her world brighter for a few weeks. He said he didn't know how she would have coped otherwise, after what had happened with our grandma. He said he's not jealous of you, only grateful that you were there when she needed it most, and happy that someone else had loved her just as he would love her when they met many years later.'

He stops there, perhaps to catch his breath and collect his thoughts. There is a look of wonder in his face, that wonder that all children share, even when they are grown up, when they discover the depths of feeling, the dense, unknown histories that make up their parents' lives. I feel an infinite tenderness inside me, filling my lungs, pressing into my heart with a pleasant ache – tenderness for this man sitting before me who suddenly looks like a child; for his sister, who is not here, who is perhaps still confused and resentful, wishing she had been told sooner, wondering whether she knew her mother at all; for their kind and loving father, who must be feeling Clara's absence now as I had done all those years ago, only a thousand times more keenly after a lifetime spent together. I think of Clara, of all the people to whom I have explained what she meant to me, all the people I tried to describe her to, just as I now know – just as I have always hoped – she had been describing me.

I find myself talking about her again, and once I've started, it is difficult to stop.

'Your mother would rescue tadpoles from the creek that ran next to her grandmother's house. Sometimes they got stranded in little shallow pools and she would scoop them out one by one, even though she found them slimy and disgusting. She said she couldn't bear to think of them flailing about in there while she slept. One time we went into town and visited this little art gallery just off the main street. It had been there for as long as I could remember, and I don't think I ever saw anyone go inside, let alone buy anything. It was run by this slightly awkward woman who aways looked like she was dressed for some kind of business conference but didn't quite know how to pick clothes that fit her right.

'We went inside because there was a painting in the window that looked interesting, and Clara wanted to see what it looked like from up close. As soon as we went in we realized it wasn't particularly good, and none of the rest of the art was any good either. I think we could tell, even at that age, that it was all cheap, generic stuff. But we still did a lap of the shop out of politeness. I'm sure it was obvious to the woman that we weren't buyers, just nosy teenagers, a waste of her time, but she still dutifully followed us around the shop, told us about the artists, asked us if there was anything we were interested in. Before we left she asked us to sign the guestbook, so of course we did. The last people who'd signed it before us had written down the date, and we could see that it had been four days since anyone had visited. I suppose it was tragic, really, though at the time I just felt awkward and embarrassed for her and just wanted to leave. But afterwards your mum was inconsolable. She felt so sorry for the lady in the shop. She kept bringing it up, trying to figure out whether she owned the place or just worked there, and what the guestbook was for. Maybe to have something to show the artists? I kept telling her not to worry about it, the shop had been there forever, so it obviously did well enough to survive. But she was sad about it for ages. Kept thinking about the lonely woman who stood there all day, in that boring shop, with her sad little guestbook and hardly any customers.'

Clara's son is smiling now, leaning forward in his chair. 'She told us about the tadpoles. She said you'd organize rescue operations together. She said you did most of the scooping out because you didn't mind the slime too much.'

'I did mind the slime, but I knew she minded it more, and I wanted to help her. I wanted her to have everything she wanted, and she only wanted good things. I know you know this already, but she really was a special person. Funny and kind and so loving. Only sometimes, she would close herself off. She would disappear into some private world that she didn't feel she could share. Then she would go quiet, like she wasn't really there.'

I stop, thinking I've said too much, but there is a look of understanding on his face, a recognition.

'She could be like that sometimes, even with us, especially when we were little. It was like the sun suddenly vanishing from the sky.'

I feel my throat tighten, my eyes sting. I know what he means. I remember it clearly.

'Afterwards,' he continues, 'she would talk to us about it, tell us she was sorry. She used to say it was important to let people into your world. When you found people you loved and who loved you, people you could trust, you did not need to hide from them. That's also how she explained how she felt about you, before she died. She said that with you she had felt she could be herself. She could tell you everything she was thinking and you would understand. She told us that whenever we found a person we felt that way about, the way she felt about our dad and maybe one or two other people in her life, and the way she had felt about you, then we should make sure to hold onto them and not be scared.'

Even now, after so many years, it is a comfort to hear these words.

'Thank you for telling me all this. Thank you for looking for me and finding me and coming all the way here,' I say to the young man who sits across from me.

He smiles a sad smile and looks like he is about to cry. There is one more thing I need to say to him, one more thing I need him to know, to tell his sister, his father.

'Your mother changed my life too. She was the first friend I ever had, maybe the best friend I ever had. She made me myself, and I never forgot her.'

He smiles again and I watch as he manages not to cry. I place my hand on his and squeeze. He squeezes back and we sit like that for a few moments. Then we let go. He asks me for pen and paper, writes down some email addresses and telephone numbers. He says that I should get in touch if I would like to, that they would be happy if they could get to know me better. He leans down to look for something in his backpack and produces an envelope. I know what it is before he even says a word.

'She wrote this for you. I think she wanted you to have it.'

He hands me the envelope, still sealed. She has written my name on it. It is still the same handwriting, only slightly older, more grown up. I thank him, and put the letter on my desk. I can feel my heart beating. Clara's son stands up and swings his backpack onto his shoulder. I stand too, walk with him the few steps to the door of my office, and then the rest of the way to the front of the building, so that I can see him off. All the time, I can feel the letter behind me, like an invisible hook in my back.

I return to my office, lock the door behind me, sit in my chair. I stare at the letter at the far corner of my desk, just out of reach.

Rosa's family home in New Saturn is more or less as she'd left it. There are signs that someone has broken in and maybe even lived there for a while – black marks where a cooking fire has been lit, some empty bottles, an old pillow. Other than that, everything is the same. But Rosa is different. It isn't just the thin scar that runs across her face or the burns on her arms: her neighbours keep saying it is something about the way she carries herself, the way she walks. She's only been gone for three years, but it might as well have been thirty. She has seen so much of the known universe that New Saturn cannot really hold her anymore. Yet as long as some part of her continues to believe that Nadia and Lynx are still alive, she knows she has to wait for them here, in the same place they found her the first time and where they might some day find her again.

Then, one day, it happens. She rounds the corner onto the street where she lives and sees Nadia and Lynx standing outside her house, trying to work out if she is in. Rosa stops in her tracks. She has dreamed of this moment every night for the past two years, and every day she has willed it into being. She has commed every rescue agency she can think of; she has scoured archives and news reports; she has even tried to contact Rowena Tawny. There have been many moments when her carefully constructed conviction that Nadia and Lynx are still alive has threatened to fall apart, or when she has feared that they might have come looking for her on New Saturn before she managed to make her way back there herself – and, not finding her there, have concluded that she has not survived the explosion that separated them. But somehow, even when loneliness and doubt threaten to overwhelm her, Rosa has managed to keep hoping. There is no alternative. She simply does not want to imagine a universe in which they no longer exist, a universe in which she will never see Nadia again.

Now that she knows she was right all along, she doesn't know what to do. She stands there, watching Lynx peering through a window while Nadia stands with one hand on her waist and the other shielding her face from the sun. Neither of them has seen her yet. Distantly, Rosa registers a clanging sound. She looks down towards the source of the noise and realizes she must have dropped her bag of work tools. When she looks back up again, Lynx and Nadia are staring at her. Nadia is wearing an eyepatch, but other than that, she looks exactly as Rosa remembers her, strong and proud and determined. And beautiful.

Rosa starts walking again. Her heart is racing, she can almost hear it, and she is aware of every sensation in her body – the weight of her arms, the feel of the ground beneath her feet, how much faster she is breathing than she normally would. Some kind of emotion is exploding inside her, something close to joy but a weird, painful kind that is more an ache, and makes her feel like she might cry. She sees Nadia looking at her as though she can't really believe what she is seeing, as though she, too, has spent so much time picturing this moment that she has no idea how to act.

Now they are standing opposite each other. Rosa raises her hand, letting her fingertips hover over Nadia's eyepatch.

'What happened to your eye?' she says.

'Just a scratch. Luckily I've got another one. What happened to your face?'

Rosa shrugs. 'No idea. It was like this when they found me. Too bad it's the only face I've got.'

Nadia lets out a sharp laugh. 'I think it suits you.'

Rosa smiles, and the tears she has been holding back

finally start to fall. Nadia gently wipes them off her cheeks. Moments later, as Lynx dances and cries with joy, and as Rosa and Nadia hug each other in the middle of the street, too happy and too stunned to say anything more, Rosa thinks to herself that this is what it must feel like to finally come home.

About the Author

Ekin Oklap was born in Turkey, grew up in Italy, and lives in London. Her translations from Turkish and Italian have been shortlisted for the International Booker Prize and John Florio Prize, among others. *First Summer* is her first novel.